THE FIRE

Daniela Krien

THE
FIRE

Translated from the German by
Jamie Bulloch

MACLEHOSE PRESS
QUERCUS · LONDON

First published in German as *Der Brand* by
Diogenes Verlag Ag, Zürich, in 2021

First published in Great Britain in 2023 by MacLehose Press

This paperback edition published in 2024 by

MacLehose Press
An imprint of Quercus Editions Limited
Carmelite House
50 Victoria Embankment
London EC4Y 0DZ

An Hachette UK company

A CIP catalogue record for this book is available from the British Library.

ISBN (MMP) 978 1 52942 140 8
ISBN (Ebook) 978 1 52942 141 5

2 4 6 8 10 9 7 5 3 1

Designed and typeset in Scala by Patty Rennie
Printed and bound in Great Britain by Clays Ltd, Elcograf S.p.A.

Contradiction is the very element
of human existence.

Ernst Cassirer

On a Friday in August, Rahel Wunderlich walks briskly down Pulsnitzer Strasse towards Martin-Luther-Platz. She feels light, almost weightless, and she breezes past most of the other pedestrians.

At the practice she sorted out her paperwork, watered the plants, and left a note with instructions for the cleaner. In her favourite bookshop she bought one title on recommendation and one by Elizabeth Strout which has been on her wishlist for a while – a mother–daughter story that's had rave reviews.

Peter should be home in an hour or so. He messaged her from a vineyard in Radebeul with photos of various bottles of Grauburgunder and Weissburgunder, and asked if she was happy with his choices. She asked for a Scheurebe too and got a curt "OK" in response.

In the entrance hall she empties her mailbox and goes through her post: a flyer from a new takeaway pizza joint, a bill from the painter who recently decorated the kitchen and a special-delivery letter from the city council: her penalty charge notice for being caught by a speed camera a few weeks ago. Ninety euros plus twenty-five for the admin fee, plus points on her licence. Could have been worse; she ran a red light too.

Rahel climbs the stairs to the second floor of the period apartment block and puts the post on the chest of drawers in the hall. As she's slipping off her shoes she hears the telephone in her room. She hesitates briefly; she really needs to pee, but she fancies she can detect an urgency in the ringing that won't wait.

□

During the call she has to sit down.

His voice cracking, the man on the telephone explains that the holiday let Rahel booked months ago has burned down. After almost a century in the family's possession, he says, the house in the mountains has been destroyed for ever.

Rahel can't muster any sympathy. As the man goes on talking, explaining about repaying the deposit and suggesting alternative accommodation, she's not thinking for a moment about the loss of the property, only about Peter and the expression on his face when he hears about this.

"So you'll take the holiday apartment in the village?" the man asks, his tone now businesslike.

"No," Rahel says. "Please refund the deposit."

□

She spent almost two months looking for a place like that. At the very start of the year, when the first reports of the virus were coming through, they'd agreed to spend the summer in Germany.

It was the perfect find: a cabin in Upper Bavaria, in the Ammergau Alps. Standing completely on its own on a grassy hill, a well with a pump and stone basin, accessible only via a bumpy, winding path through the woods. No internet, no television, no distractions.

Peter has been poring over maps for weeks, putting together hiking routes. He's bought expensive walking boots, a daypack, T-shirts and trousers made from quick-dry and rain-resistant material, a top-notch jacket from a Swiss firm and special supportive socks. Rahel has kitted herself out expensively too, and she's been exercising almost every day in preparation for their hikes.

They would have been leaving in three days. They'll never be able to find something similar at such short notice, not this year, not in the circumstances. Without much expectation she enters her requests on a holiday apartment website. No matches. She tries again on another site – with the same result.

Rahel goes to the website with the Alpine cabin. She clicks from picture to picture, from the geraniums in the window boxes to the small veranda with a view of the mountain range opposite, and back to the house, this time from a different angle. Then the stone basin by the well and the colourful wildflower meadow, and all of a sudden she can picture the blazing fire on the mountain. She sees animals fleeing, a column of smoke rising into a night sky studded with stars, and in the middle of it all Peter and herself, as if on a funeral pyre.

▢

Had this happened ten years ago the two of them would have shaken their heads. "Who knows, there might be a silver lining . . ." Peter would have probably said, giving her a comforting hug. But he's not so laid back anymore. His subtle sense of humour often veers towards the cynical nowadays, and their lively discussions have given way to a polite amicability. But, worst of all, he's stopped sleeping with her.

▢

It's been half an hour since the phone call. Rahel is standing barefoot at her bedroom window, bobbing up and down on the balls of her feet. Her black hair, streaked with grey, is pinned up. As if from a distance she takes in the world outside, the voices of the teenagers who've gathered on the benches by the church. The disappointment has left her feeble.

When the phone rings again she doesn't budge. She closes her eyes and waits for it to stop.

But it doesn't.

She glances at the screen: it's Ruth. Rahel instinctively tenses her shoulders, clears her throat, checks the expression on her face in the mirror beside the desk and lifts the receiver.

She can immediately detect the change in Ruth's voice, which is lacking its snappy confidence. But she comes straight to the point: Viktor had a stroke a few days ago. It's all been too much, which is why she hasn't rung till now. Today he was admitted to the rehabilitation clinic in Ahrenshoop, where he's going to spend the next six weeks. A place unexpectedly became free. Ruth says she wants to go and give him support; she's already organised to stay with their mutual friend Frauke, a painter who lives in Ahrenshoop. Now she's looking for someone to mind the house and animals in Dorotheen-felde. She's not normally one to ask but . . .

She breaks off, then starts again: would Rahel and Peter be able to do the first two weeks? Viktor and she would be incredibly grateful.

Rahel almost says *No. No, I'm afraid we can't. We're going to the mountains.* But then she remembers the fire and says, "Yes, of course, we'd be delighted to. We'll stay three weeks if you like."

□

Peter is silent. He shakes his head and throws his hands in the air, utterly baffled.

"That's impossible!" he says finally. "What is the probability of booking the one holiday house that burns down just before you're about to go there?"

Then he shuffles off to his room, head bowed. It used to be Selma's bedroom. When she moved out Simon got an upgrade, and when it was his turn to leave the parental nest, Peter took it. Simon's old room is the guest room and what used to be Peter's study is now Rahel's. They reorganised the apartment as soon as Simon moved out. For a while they looked for somewhere smaller, but everything that came up was more expensive, despite the location never being as good. Here they are on the borders of Äussere Neustadt and Radeberger Vorstadt, which means they can easily get to both the Elbwiesen and Dresden Heath; they didn't want that to change.

For now, Rahel breathes a sigh of relief. She doesn't yet know how to tell him what she's promised Ruth. She goes to the window, leans out, looks down at the passers-by and suddenly hears Peter's voice behind her.

"So, what are we going to do now?" he says. He sits down on the midnight-blue chaise longue that Rahel bought recently.

She hesitates with her answer, but finally her pragmatism wins over.

"We'll go to the Uckermark, to Dorotheenfelde, tomorrow."

Her smile slips and she can't hold his gaze. As she stares at her painted toenails she tells him about Ruth's call. Peter makes a noise that sounds as if he's choking.

"Without consulting me . . ." he says, getting up. "So that's where we've got to, is it?"

She feels as if her feet are stuck to the floor and her tongue to the roof of her mouth. Peter leaves the room with a look of defeat on his face.

Rahel sits on the chaise longue, exactly where he was perched. Then she stretches out and covers her eyes with her arm. She looks inwards and immediately wishes she hadn't.

□

Later, as she's taking clothes out of the wardrobe at random and packing them into the suitcase, she thinks of Ruth. She can see her face vividly. Over the years tiny shifts may have crept into the symmetry of those features, but Ruth still dresses immaculately. Especially on bad days, her external perfection is her defence against the weight of the world. This attitude seems to have rubbed off on Rahel since as long as she can remember. In Ruth's presence she has never let herself go, never dressed or moved sloppily. Ruth absorbed this unquestioned discipline during her years at the Palucca School. She and Rahel's mother Edith began their training in classical dance at the same time, when they were children. Edith chucked it in after three years; Ruth stuck with it. The girls remained friends into adulthood.

Rahel's relationship to Viktor and Ruth is seamless and as old as she is. Her life always settled down when she stayed with them in Dorotheenfelde. Edith's restless existence, which gave Rahel and her sister Tamara a childhood with a suc-cession of stepfathers, endless moves throughout the length and breadth of Dresden and a number of different schools, was like a storm on the high seas, and although Dorotheen-felde never became a permanent port, it provided beneficial lulls.

Edith and Ruth were inseparable during those days in

Dorotheenfelde. Despite their differences, the friends' bond was close and when a few years ago cancer took hold of Edith's body for the third and last time, Ruth came and stayed. Until the end.

□

They drive all the way without stopping. The satnav had estimated three hours and thirteen minutes; Peter thought that was a good time.

On the way she calls the children and puts her phone on speaker. Selma is carrying whiny Max. His screeching drowns out Selma's voice.

"How dreadful that you've got to go somewhere else on holiday now, Mum!" she shouts down the phone. "If I get a minute to myself around midnight I'll make sure I feel sorry for you." She hangs up.

Peter immediately tries to calm the situation. "Leave her! She's got two small children to look after."

"She's got a husband who'll do anything for her."

"Sounds like you're envious."

Rahel decides to drop the subject and calls Simon.

"Bet he doesn't answer," Peter says, grinning. It's the first smile in days and although she doesn't like the reason for it, she feels happier. After the thirteenth ring she hangs up.

"Why does he bother having a phone?" she grumbles.

"He'll be somewhere in the mountains."

Rahel nods and drops the mobile into her bag.

□

They drive through the village, then take a right turn onto a track. The cul-de-sac sign is faded and crooked. Viktor drove into it a few times before finally surrendering his licence.

They judder along the paving stones, grass growing up in the middle, then the paving comes to an end too and they continue on gravel and sand up the slight incline.

Ruth is waiting for them outside. Tall, upright and in a low-cut dress that emphasises her impressive breasts. No hint of infirmity even though she's almost seventy now. Rahel gets out and walks over to her, while Peter drives on to park the car.

The stable is attached to the left of the main house; to the right is a large barn. Refugees lived here after the war, and later the farm was the headquarters of the local agricultural cooperative. After that, Viktor and Ruth, along with two other families, lived in the former manager's house, which had a stove heater and outdoor privy. The first family moved away in the early seventies and the other left at the beginning of the eighties.

After reunification Viktor and Ruth bought the property, which by now was semi-derelict, and renovated it bit by bit over many years. Now it's starting to crumble again.

Ruth wriggles out of their embrace. "I'm all sweaty," she says, and wanders off to greet Peter.

A carafe of water, a plate with cake and a fly cover and a thermos flask stand on the garden table. Ruth pours coffee and begins to talk about Viktor. As she speaks Rahel wonders whether she'll ever speak so lovingly about Peter. Ruth's words emit a profound closeness, and Rahel can feel Peter's eyes on her.

▫

After finishing their coffee they fetch the luggage from the car and follow Ruth up the steps. On the first floor she points to a room at the end of the landing on the right.

"You'd be best off sleeping in there, in the north-east-facing room. It's nice and cool. Although . . ." she says, pointing in the opposite direction, ". . . you could take the south-west-facing one. You can see the lake glistening between the trees. But I don't need to tell you any of this, you know your way around here."

Ruth turns and goes back down the stairs.

Without exchanging glances they go their own ways – Peter to the north-east, Rahel to the south-west. They close their doors quietly.

◻

Later Ruth gives them instructions. Just watering the plants will take at least an hour a day. They should use the water butts around the house.

Viktor's studio is at the front of the barn, but they don't go in. In recent years, Ruth says, his works have become smaller. His physical strength may have waned, but his technical skill and imagination are as strong as ever.

The animals are the hardest part. Neither Peter nor Rahel have looked after animals before. Now they're going to be responsible for the welfare of a horse, some cats, a dozen chickens and a white stork that can't fly.

They stroll around the entire property. One window in the stable must be kept open at all times to allow the swallows to fly in and out unhindered. In the chicken garden behind the stable the apple trees are bearing ripe fruit. The wire-mesh fence has been patched up in places. Everywhere they look, they see work that could be done. The countless roses growing up the wall of the barn in the courtyard haven't been pruned in ages, the creeping vine beneath the projecting roof of the stables has withered, Rahel counts three broken windows on their tour, and leaves and twigs from last year still lie all over the place.

Ruth acts as if everything is fine.

Suddenly she looks up at the sky.

"Seven o'clock," she says. "Suppertime."

□

They eat at an attractively laid table in the yard as the onset of darkness swallows the signs of decay. There is solyanka, bread, red wine and water, and in a moment of profound contentment Peter says in a thick Saxonian accent, "Impeccable!"

Ruth bursts out laughing, which infects Rahel too, and both repeat the word in unison: "Impeccable". A memory flashes in Rahel's mind.

Not that long ago, two years perhaps, they were also sitting here and laughing, with Viktor, Ruth and Simon, and there was solyanka, bread and wine. Simon turned down a drink and when questioned by Viktor he explained why. Rahel and Peter knew already. After studying sports science at the army university their son was planning to qualify as a mountain ranger, which would require two or three years of preparation. The training included elite-level climbing and skiing in impassable terrain high up in the Alps and in the worst weather conditions, as well as endurance and mental strength. For him it all began with giving up alcohol. Rahel had already been horrified by her son's decision to pursue an officer's commission in the army. His ambition to become the leader of a mountain unit was another shock, and she was not reassured by his claim that the whole thing was more like a sporting challenge. That afternoon Viktor had been equally sceptical. "And if needs be you'll put your head on the line for this country?" he said in disbelief. "Nobody will reward you for that."

□

She finds Ruth uncanny sometimes. As if her friend were able to read Rahel's thoughts, she suddenly asks about Simon.

"Still at the army university in Munich," Peter replies.

"He hasn't called me back yet, our would-be officer," Rahel mutters with an anxious glance at her mobile. Then she clicks on the Photos app to show pictures of her children and grandchildren, but Ruth's comments are no more than pleasantries. At the right moments she says in a deep voice, *Oh* and *How nice* and *I see*, but her gaze keeps wandering and her laughter doesn't sound genuine. Yawning behind a hand, she tells them she plans to leave early.

"You don't have to get up with me. Let's say our goodbyes now and be done with it," she says with her usual assertiveness.

Week One

Monday

When Rahel wakes up it's almost eight o'clock. She must have turned off the alarm but she can't remember. She didn't get much sleep; Simon answered her message only at around one a.m.

Hi Mum, really sorry Bavaria hasn't worked out. I deffo would've come along and shown you a few nice trails. Oh well, another time! I'm fine. Training in the Karwendel mountains. Hi to all! Simon

She was relieved for now, but she knew full well that the risks would never go away. The demons that tormented Rahel at night offered up images of his crushed body.

They turn up to her practice from time to time – the mother whose only child was run over while crossing the road, or the father who watched his daughter drown in the Baltic. They sit facing her like lights that have gone out, lacking any joy for life and lacking the energy to put an end to it.

Rahel gets up, goes into the bathroom next door and removes the night guard from her mouth. She too would become one of those burnt-out individuals if one of her children died. She dismisses the thought, cleans the guard, puts it in the plastic box and drinks from the tap. Back in the bedroom she swaps her nightie for a black linen dress and looks out of the window. A figure goes into the woods, heading for the lake. Rahel fetches her glasses from the bedside table and peers out again. The person has vanished from sight, and all she can see is the stork trudging along behind the house, its head drawn in.

□

"Snakes, mice, moles. Live, of course," Ruth had said with a straight face when Rahel asked what the stork ate. After savouring their expressions of bewilderment, she allowed a smile to dart across her lips. "But you can also give it the little fish that are in the fridge. Or the chicks and mice in the freezer. And if it ever rains again you can collect snails from the lupins and hostas."

The bird has no name.

Rahel wanders barefoot down the long landing to Peter's room. She knocks, waits, knocks again, then goes in. The windows are wide open and she hears the sparrows making a racket in the elder bush whose branches almost reach into the room. His bed is empty, the duvet neatly folded. She sits on the edge and runs her hand beneath the duvet to feel for his warmth. But the sheet is smooth and cool.

He's piled the books he intends to read on the desk: *Propaganda* by Steffen Kopetzky, the first volume of Ricarda Huch's *In the Old Reich. Sketches of German Cities*, the collected essays of Montaigne, Tomas Tranströmer's complete poems, Pier Paolo Pasolini's *Corsair Writings* and Ernst Jünger's *The Forest Passage*.

In the middle of the desk is a freshly sharpened pencil on a new notebook, behind it his glasses and a packet of tissues. For some reason this careful arrangement touches her deeply. She goes out of the room without leaving any trace and saunters downstairs.

16

Rahel feels somewhat at a loss as she enters the kitchen. What she would give now for a cappuccino from her machine at home, complete with frothy milk and a little brown sugar. She walks around, opening cupboards, and gradually pieces together the order behind Ruth's apparent chaos. There is no coffee machine, just a cafetière. Ruth and Viktor are passionate devotees of green tea. Peter noted to his delight the large selection of pots, teas and cups soon after they arrived.

She rinses the cafetière with hot water and finds some coffee in a black tin. Rahel gives it a sniff; it seems fresh. Then she hears the door close followed by Peter's footsteps in the hallway. He enters in good spirits and tells her about his swim in the lake.

"Oh, so you were the person in the woods," she says.

He nods. "I was the only swimmer in that entire huge lake."

"Shall I make you a cup of tea?" she asks, laying a hand on his arm.

"No, I'll do it."

Peter is thrilled to discover that the kettle has temperature settings, so it's simple to make tea with water at 70 degrees. Meanwhile Rahel cooks porridge. They divide up the tasks. To her amazement, Peter, who has never been interested in animals and always stubbornly rejected the children's pleas for a pet, announces:

"I'll look after the animals."

Rahel's pleased. She prefers the garden.

Peter hurriedly leaves the breakfast table. She sees him heading for the stable, from where he reappears soon afterwards with the bridled horse.

The horse is a twenty-three-year-old sorrel mare called Baila. For the past five years she's been enjoying her dotage here having had to retire from showjumping after an injury.

She plods behind Peter, seemingly reluctant to move to the paddock. Baila keeps stopping, setting her ears back and digging her hooves into the ground. Pulling and coaxing have no effect. Suddenly Peter grabs the halter rope, spins it around and gives the obstinate Baila a lash on the hindquarters. At once she gets moving and duly walks behind him.

A little later Rahel watches him feeding the stork, which has its fish served up in a plastic bowl and greedily sets about its breakfast. Ruth let the chickens out and fed them before she left, and the cats seem to be full and content too. They're lying about, roaming the yard, or stealing via a cat flap into the house, where they disperse on the ground floor.

Leaving the dishes in the kitchen, Rahel wanders outside. She picks up one of the watering cans but the butts are empty. In this region, too, summers are getting hotter, drier and dustier. The spruces and beeches in the woods are dying, and in August it already looks like autumn. She turns on the tap by the front door, unwinds the hose and starts watering those plants she reckons have the best chance of survival. Hibiscus, rosebushes, a rhododendron, a variety of hydrangeas, marigolds and hostas are drooping limply, but perk up again after a while. Only the lavender is thriving without any help, forming wonderfully fragrant islands. How Ruth, soon to be seventy, and her eighty-year-old husband manage to keep on top of the house, garden and animals is a mystery to her. She can't begin to imagine what will happen if Viktor doesn't get better.

Peter is busy until lunchtime. Rahel has emptied the contents of the vegetable drawer onto the table, chucked away what was rotten and made a soup from the rest. There's still plenty of bread. She sets the table outside, puts up the umbrella, dips the clay wine cooler in water until it darkens and chooses a Weissburgunder from the bottles they brought.

In the fridge she finds two lamb sausages, both of which she leaves for Peter with a sigh. For a while now she's been eating less to keep her figure.

Over lunch Peter says he's planning a longer walk with Baila in the afternoon. Ruth asked him to exercise the mare for at least an hour per day. He doesn't look at Rahel, nor does he ask if she'd like to come with him.

When they're clearing up he drops a glass, which smashes on the flagstones outside the door. Peter freezes, staring at the shards scattered on the ground. He doesn't move for several seconds, he just looks, and it's this expression that stops her from helping him. Rahel turns away. A ray of sun hits her face and she closes her eyes. When she opens them he's squatting on the ground, sweeping the shards with a brush.

□

Peter sets off with Baila; Rahel wanders around the house which has stood here for more than a hundred and fifty years. Like an organism with its own laws, it keeps admitting new people, enveloping them, absorbing them, permeating them, working first in them, then through them.

Deep scratches scar the light wooden floor, some of the terracotta tiles in the kitchen are cracked or chipped and there are no clear surfaces. Everything horizontal is covered – every windowsill, every chest, every table carries piles of newspaper articles, exhibition catalogues, books, photos, CDs, notes, sketches and hosts of carved figures for the children Ruth never gave birth to.

Rahel spots those that Viktor made for her years ago. She picks up one of them – an elf – and takes it on her tour.

When the phone rings in the corridor she hesitates. Ruth didn't leave any instructions for possible calls. The phone is new. The instruction booklet and till receipt are lying next to it. Before the answerphone can kick in she picks up.

"Hello, Rahel," Ruth says. "It's me. I've arrived safely and Viktor sends his love. He said it three times; it seems to be extremely important to him."

"Thanks! How is he?"

"Alright, considering. Listen, I've got to go because a doctor's coming to discuss the therapy programme. Just quickly, how are the animals?"

"Fine! Excellent! Don't you worry, we've got everything under control."

"I'm so glad. I'll call again. Bye, bye, sweetheart and say hi to Peter."

"I will."

When Ruth hangs up Rahel remembers all the questions she ought to have asked. Where's the hoover? What day are the bins collected? Should I forward your post? For a moment she just stands there by the telephone, then she slips the elf into the pocket of her dress, goes outside, crosses the yard and opens the door to Viktor's studio.

At the far end of the room, out of reach of the sunlight, is a life-size sculpture on a pedestal. A naked woman, her legs slightly apart, torso and arms arched backwards. A dancer's pose or an expression of intense pain. Stepping closer, Rahel gets a shock: between the legs, right beneath the pubic region, a large spider has spun a web. At once disgusted and fascinated, Rahel watches the animal, which quickly retreats.

She fetches a chair so she can take a closer look at the sculpture's face. Ruth, no doubt about it. Not Ruth now but Ruth as a young woman, Ruth before she got married, as a dancer, as the muse of the artist Viktor Kolbe.

On the wall to the right hang his chisels in a neat row. There must be a hundred of them. On a workbench is an open box with carving tools and beside it a few unfinished works, almost all of which appear religious. There is a book too: *The Way of a Pilgrim*. On a piece of paper it says in Viktor's expressive handwriting: *Pray without ceasing!* And *Lord Jesus Christ, have mercy on me.*

Astonished, Rahel leafs through the pilgrim book. As far as she knows Viktor isn't religious.

She puts it back and leaves the studio in a strangely glum mood.

◻

From her room she fetches a towel, puts it around her shoulders and makes for the lake. Young voices drift over to her from a bathing spot on the other side, but here she is alone. She swims naked, as usual. The cool, clean water envelops her body, and it is this moment of immersion that she loves, when the sounds of the world disappear and she's surrounded by total silence.

On the way back she tries to imagine what they would be doing in Bavaria now. But nothing comes to mind.

Peter is sitting in the shade on a bench in the yard. He's pulled his hat down over his face, crossed his arms and seems to be dozing. As she approaches he raises his head.

They sit side by side without touching. When he tells Rahel about his walk with Baila he makes her laugh. To start with the mare acted as if she were lame. She kept stopping, tossing her head or trying to nibble the grass beside the path. But then on the way back she broke into a trot and Peter had trouble keeping up with her.

Just as Rahel is about to tell him what she found in the

21

studio he stands up and says, "I'm going to have a bit of a lie down."

"Fine," she says, without meaning it.

□

Before supper Rahel studs two lemon halves with cloves and puts them on the table outside to keep the wasps away. In the fridge she finds a bit of cured beef, a small, soft goat's cheese and a few olives. They'll have to go shopping tomorrow.

She fancies some red wine, but the prospect of a bad night's sleep puts her off.

Rahel carries out the tray with the cutlery and crockery, sets the table and sees Peter coming out of the front door. He's carrying three large tins of cat food which he shares between several bowls. Then he steps back a few paces and watches the mob as they eat. A smaller cat with reddish-brown fur, who's missing an ear, tries in vain to get to the food. Peter shoos away the others, picks up one of the bowls, grabs the little cat and takes her to where she can eat in peace under his protection.

"You're upsetting the pecking order," Rahel calls over to him. He nods, looking quite pleased.

□

After supper he pushes his plate to the middle of the table, takes a gulp of beer, puts the bottle down, stretches his legs and crosses his hands behind his head – a pose that Rahel has seen many men assume, but never Peter.

"It's actually good that Bavaria didn't work out, don't you think?" he says, and although this thought has crossed her mind too she says, "No. I don't know what's good about it."

He gives her a serious look. Then he sits up, quickly finishes his beer and begins to clear the table.

◻

Rahel sits outside until her eyes have become accustomed to the darkness. The moon casts sufficient light on the yard for her to be able to see outlines and the numerous bats flitting past. Today and for the next few days the Perseid meteor shower is at its peak. She'd love to gaze up at the sky with Peter now, and maybe, later, sleep with him.

His refusal tortures her.

◻

Even before the incident at the university Rahel had become wary. It was the way they had sex and the fact that she was almost always the one taking the initiative – she knew the signs. So many of her clients had told her how their sex lives had gone adrift. Love had turned into loving friendship and it was hardly ever possible to reverse this.

Sometimes straight after orgasm Peter would begin talking about whatever topic was on his mind. At other times he would give her such strangely insipid looks, looks devoid of any desire, which made her body go limp. At the first signs of menopause she was thrown into textbook mood swings. There were moments when, filled with lust, she would ring Peter at the university and entice him home. On other days she couldn't bear to be touched by him. Sometimes she wanted him several times on the same day, and when he began to evade her desire she asked him anxiously if he was having an affair.

"My God, Rahel!" he said. "To start with I don't find it particularly arousing to have someone throw themselves at me, and second, there are people for whom sex doesn't have the same meaning!"

That hit home. She went into a huff for a few weeks and

for a while she considered hormone treatment to mitigate the severe mood swings. But, if she was being truthful, she wanted to feel it all. The tears that seemed to come from nowhere, the exhaustion, the sweating, the euphoria at simply being alive and the hunger for her husband.

Sometimes it wasn't the hunger for him, but the desire for any man.

Tuesday

Judging by the position of the sun it must be late morning. She's overslept again and it feels as if she's stolen a portion of her own life.

She pulls on the black linen dress she wore yesterday and suspects she'll be wearing it for the next few days too. As she dresses, the elf rolls out of her pocket and falls on the floor. A wing has broken off. She lays it carefully on the bedside table, stands the figure beside it and thinks of Viktor. His interest in Rahel was conspicuous, especially compared to her sister Tamara, to whom he was rather indifferent. When Ruth once picked him up on this he said curtly that Tamara had a father whereas Rahel didn't.

☐

There's cold tea in the kitchen. No sign of Peter, which just now is a relief. She makes coffee, spreads jam on a roll and eats it standing up. Without being able to say why, she feels drawn again to Viktor's studio. She crosses the yard carefully with her full cup of coffee and heads straight for the work-bench where the book is. *Lord Jesus Christ, have mercy on me.* Rahel utters the prayer, each time stressing it differently until she's found a rhythm: *Lord Jesus Christ, have mercy on me, Lord Jesus Christ, have mercy on me, Lord Jesus Christ, have mercy on me, Lord Jesus Christ, have mercy on me, Lord Jesus Christ, have mercy on me.*

She doesn't feel anything.

Beside the workbench is a cabinet. In the top drawer are charcoal sketches of animals, mainly horses and cats. In the second drawer Rahel finds a variety of pencils, a cardboard box with charcoal sticks, sketchpads, a pouch of tobacco and papers, candles and lighters. The tobacco is still moist; it can't be old. Does Ruth know about it?

She opens another drawer: a number of drawings of a female torso in different poses. Rahel looks through them one by one. Most are rapid sketches; only a few look as if they've been fleshed out. The last one has a head and a face. It is Edith, Rahel's mother.

Next to these is another pile of drawings featuring a child, and this child is her.

Rahel stares at these pictures for several minutes. The contents of these drawers were not meant to be seen by anyone. She feels like a thief, but at the same time like someone who's had property withheld from them.

Her hands trembling, Rahel takes the tobacco from the other drawer. Pulling out a paper she rolls her first cigarette in more than twenty years. But before she can light it she hears hooves on the cobbles in the yard and, when she peers out of the window a moment later, Baila comes into view. The mare stops, paws the ground a few times with her right front hoof and snorts. The halter rope is dangling and she can't see Peter anywhere. Rahel puts the cigarette on the table and hurries outside.

Peter comes trudging up to the barn about five minutes later, shaking his head and laughing.

"I had to tie my laces and before I knew it she'd done a runner."

Grabbing the halter rope he begins to give Baila a lecture.

If only he spoke half as much to me, Rahel thinks, watching him lead the mare to the paddock.

◻

After a quick dip in the lake Rahel heads back into the house. She hopes to find Peter in his room. What she discovered in the studio is bothering her; she feels uneasy about the questions it's thrown up, and the only person who can answer them is in a rehabilitation clinic by the Baltic Sea, being watched over by his wife.

But she wants to talk to Peter about something else.

She ties her hair up the way he likes it, pulls a few of the looser strands out to the side, applies a touch of lipstick, puts on some mascara and looks at herself in the mirror for a while. On good days you can't tell she's forty-nine.

With every step towards his room she goes more cautiously. The old floorboards creak and just as she's about to knock he calls out, "Come in."

Seated at his desk in front of an open book, he turns to her and takes off his glasses.

"Peter, what's happened to us?"

He points to the chair beside his bed. "Sit down."

Cold beads of sweat run from her armpits as she scans his face. She can see he's struggling for words.

"Peter, please!"

"You've rather caught me on the hop, Rahel. I don't want to say anything wrong, I . . . Could we discuss this later? This afternoon?"

With dignified composure Rahel gets up and goes to the door. She manages a weary smile before heading for her room down the long landing.

For the past year and four months Peter has spent most of the time on his own. He's good at it. He'll read different translations of a particular book for comparison, watch nature programmes, documentaries about historical figures or travelogues, go on long bike rides to the wineries around Dresden or spend weeks studying a carefully chosen topic, which he'll examine from a literary, artistic and academic perspective. His penchant for thoroughness verges on pedantry; his critical distance has become a renunciation of the world.

He came home earlier that Thursday, the day when his already fragile equilibrium reached a tipping point. She hadn't been expecting him. When she came out of the shower wearing only a towel he was standing like a statue in the corridor. His half-absent, half-horrified expression wasn't a good sign, and she realised straightaway that the evening would turn out differently from how she'd hoped. It was their wedding anniversary, their twenty-eighth.

"What's up?" she asked, unable to disguise the faint irritation in her voice. Too often when he got home lately *something had been up*. On an almost daily basis he was appalled by the number of students struggling with spelling and grammar, and shocked by how poorly read and historically clueless they were.

Rahel rolled her eyes at these gripes. Her pragmatism had no time for pointless outrage, and although she realised how such things grieved people like Peter, she had little patience for it.

"Come on," she said in response to his silence. "Why don't I open a bottle of wine?"

He shook his head. In the kitchen he poured himself a glass of water and drank it.

"This isn't my world anymore, Rahel," he said, staring out of the window.

She spent the next half hour with him at the kitchen table, her hair wet and her feet cold. With gruelling precision he told her about the incident, and Rahel sat with her legs tucked up, listening to him.

In a seminar on the topic of "gender roles in nineteenth-century literature" Peter had handed out an extensive reading list. A few students had objected to the length of the list, arguing that all it did was offer up male and female clichés. Binary classifications which nobody believed in anymore. You only needed to read one of these books, they said, or a few extracts, and you would know it all. Peter countered that reading mere extracts or a single example was inadequate for the requirements of a university education. And even if, after all the reading, it turned out that there was a preponderance of outdated clichés, this would throw up exciting questions. They could ask themselves whether there was truth to be found in the clichés too. They could develop and discuss hypotheses. He posited the thesis that women frequently prioritised different values and objectives in life from men. They were often averse to an unadulterated thirst for power, for example, which was a welcome contrast to all those male narcissists in positions of power. At that moment there was uproar from a small group of students, the like of which he'd never come across in all his years of teaching.

One person in particular had challenged him vociferously: Olivia P.

He was an insidious chauvinist, she said, because he was praising women for not being power-hungry instead of encouraging their ambitions to take power. Intervening immediately, Peter addressed her as Frau P., at which she

29

hurled at him an angry "I'm non-binary!" For a moment he was actually lost for words, then he looked at his seminar list and remarked that he had her down as *Frau Olivia P.* Olivia P. exploded. Was he refusing to accept that she was neither the one nor the other? Not at all, he replied, all he'd said was that he had her on his list as Frau— The rest was drowned out by shouting.

Peter described what had happened down to the last, tiny detail.

"Good God!" Rahel eventually interrupted him. "Although sometimes you can be a bit of a . . ." She almost called him a nit-picker, but caught herself just in time and went on: "Who knows what kind of a sorry life that poor person's had. Just call her how she wants to be called!"

He looked at her with unfamiliar eyes. A nerve twitched in his face. Then he got up and went to his room, closing the door quietly behind him.

From then on there was silence between them and she was not aware of what happened afterwards. It was only when she came across an article in one of the major national dailies that she realised just how serious the issue had become: "Fossils. German professor at TU Dresden refuses to recognise non-binary identity of transgender student." What followed was an attack on the former East. Those individuals who'd been indoctrinated in the past had not yet learned how to think openly and freely. Their shortcomings were superbly exemplified by Prof. Wunderlich and so on, and so on. All the ghastly shit none of them could listen to anymore.

She cancelled her morning appointments and drove to the university.

Peter was in his office. He'd turned his chair and was gazing out of the window, his arms on the armrests.

"Oh, it's you," was all he said when she hurried over to give him a hug.

□

Then Oliva P. unleashed a shitstorm on social media.

To begin with Peter reacted with almost detached incomprehension. Not only did he refrain from defending himself, he didn't respond to any of the things that had kicked off on Facebook, Twitter and Co either. But he'd underestimated the dynamism of events. Soon there were posters in the university corridors with pictures of him and words from his lectures and seminars taken out of context.

The dean and the vice dean of the faculty accused him of dealing clumsily with Olivia P. His observation that she had been listed as a woman was an unnecessary provocation, they maintained, and the students' protest was perfectly legitimate in a democracy. Everyone was required to play their part in the progression towards a language free of discrimination. Peter should let the dust settle, and be more prudent in future.

"Do you know what the worst thing about this whole affair is?" he said in a weary voice, before immediately giving the answer: "It's that you've stabbed me in the back."

□

Rahel is lying on the bed in her room. That cigarette is waiting out in the studio, and now's the right time to smoke it. She sits up and stretches her back. On the way downstairs she remembers the fridge is almost empty and that the bread won't last until tomorrow. Turning back, she knocks on Peter's door again, waits for his answer then opens it a crack.

"I'm just popping to the shops. Want anything?"

"No. Actually . . ." He turns to her. ". . . a bit of smoked fish would be nice. Char or eel, or whatever they've got."

She nods. And feels happy that there's something he wants.

Rahel drives off very slowly. Less than twenty metres from the house she spots the boulder, an erratic which had seemed gigantic when she was a child. One time Viktor lifted her onto it and told her how the stone had been transported by a glacier around fifteen thousand years ago and was left there when the ice melted. He said that the lake had been formed by glacier water too, in fact the entire landscape with its gentle hills was the result of the last ice age. *Terminal moraine.* A term she desperately tried to remember. But she'd also found it yucky that the lake she swam in was supposed to be fifteen thousand years old.

"I'm not going in water that's as old as that," she declared to Ruth and her mother afterwards, and she was deeply offended when they burst out laughing.

The boulder still looks imposing but, like everything that can be classified and understood, it no longer radiates magic.

◻

It takes her a good quarter of an hour to get to the grocery. She does a big shop to avoid having to leave the house again for a while, and on the way back stops at the fishmongers in the village. She buys smoked char and eel, and also asks for scraps for the stork, which the fishmonger gives her for nothing. Then she drives swiftly back to the farmhouse.

◻

Peter is sitting beneath the open umbrella at the table, talking to the stork. From time to time the bird flaps its useless wings but doesn't move from Peter's side. When she switches off the engine the two of them go over to her. Peter opens the boot and begins to take the shopping into the kitchen. The stork stays beside the car.

"I've got fish," she says inside, taking the packet out of the bag. "Eel and char, nice and fresh."

"Marvellous." He smiles. "Did you remember Mr Stork too?"

By way of an answer she holds up the bag with the fish scraps.

"Marvellous," he says again affably, taking the bag from her hand and going outside.

Rahel sits down at the kitchen table for a moment. She suddenly feels very tired.

She looks out of the window. The sun has passed its peak. The stork is greedily getting stuck into its food while Peter keeps the cats away. Rahel isn't hungry, and nor does she fancy cooking. So after putting away the shopping she scurries across the yard into the studio.

□

Just as she's about to light the cigarette Peter opens the door and noses in.

"I've been looking for you. Shall I make us a salad? We could have the fish with it."

"Yes, lovely!" she says quickly.

"Will you make your wonderful dressing? I don't know how to."

She surreptitiously drops the cigarette behind the books on the workbench and follows him into the kitchen.

Peter switches on the radio, listens to the newsreader for a few seconds, groans, shakes his head and looks for a different station. Passing over old hits, pop and squealy ads, he stops at a recording of the Trout Quintet.

"That's better," he says, and sets about washing the salad.

Rahel puts oil, vinegar, mustard, honey, lemon juice, pepper and salt into a small bowl. With a small whisk she beats the ingredients until they come together and thicken, then she tastes with her finger. She's happy with it. Contrasts are what makes food delicious – sweet and salt, sweet and spicy, sweet and sour. Glancing at Peter, she wonders why he can't see that their differences are what constitute the attraction between them. As parents they interlock like a pair of cogwheels to form a well-functioning family mechanism the children can always rely on. But Rahel must take care she doesn't bubble over. She mustn't let her unbridled vivacity steam ahead. For then he'll retreat into his shell like a snail and wait. In literature he loves impatient, tempestuous souls. Only in books does he get close to them without feeling threatened.

She takes a knife and chopping board, and sits at the table with him. The way Peter cuts the cucumber, meticulously and into pieces almost exactly the same size, is how he approaches everything. There's no difference between plan and execution; words and deeds dependably correspond. It was this mentality that Rahel fell in love with almost thirty years ago. After all the chaos that had gone before it was like falling into a soft, warm bed.

He scrapes the chopped cucumber and pepper into the salad bowl, unwraps the fish from the paper and puts it on a white china platter, then fetches plates, cutlery, white wine and glasses.

"Weren't we going to eat outside?" Rahel asks, but she already knows the answer.

"Better not. The wasps."

Rahel gives the faintest of nods. "Water's supposed to help," she says softly.

He raises his eyebrows.

"Water from a spray bottle. It makes them think it's raining."

"Or," he says, "we can have a relaxed lunch in here and then have a coffee outside."

"OK."

The victory of reason doesn't make her happy. She eats without appetite, leaves the dishes to Peter and says she's going up to her room for an afternoon rest.

"You wanted to talk . . ." he says. It's somewhere between a question and a statement.

She can only manage a tired nod.

"Shall we meet outside the front at three and go for a little walk?"

There is such affection in his voice that Rahel almost bursts into tears.

□

At three on the dot Rahel steps out of the front door. Her eyes sweep the yard. Peter is sitting on one of the many benches dotted around the place. He's wearing his Panama hat and the one-eared cat is on his lap. When Rahel wanders over to him he carefully lifts the cat from his knees and stands up.

They take the track through the woods down to the lake, but then turn onto a bigger path – an old sunken lane that Rahel loved when she was a girl. It's a silken day. A soft, warm wind caresses her bare arms and legs. Peter adjusts his glasses and nudges his hat up.

"Do you want to go first? I'll listen."

Although she spent the whole of her afternoon rest polishing her speech, it's all gone now. She desperately tries to remember her opening sentences. Peter walks patiently alongside her. She slaps a mosquito on her neck, grabs Peter's arm and stops.

"Do you really still want to be with me?"

It's out now. At this point the sunken lane is so deep that the embankments on either side allow for no view of the countryside beyond. Above them the boughs of the trees grow together, forming a thick canopy.

He looks at her in horror, then hangs his head.

"It's a simple question, Peter. You ought to be able to answer it."

His eyes meet hers.

"What about you? Would you have had a clear answer to that question at every point in our marriage?"

She hesitates, spots two mosquitoes on her arm, and goes for them lightning fast.

"Come on, let's keep going," he says, setting off again. "I don't want to break up with you, Rahel. But right now I can't live with you the way you need me to."

"What are you talking about?"

"Full on."

"What's that supposed to mean?" she asks acidly, stepping in his path again.

He flinches. "You know exactly what I mean."

Yes, she does. But she's not going to spare him from saying it out loud.

She insists her clients name the problem they come to her with. If something can't be put into language, there's no way it will be solved. The same is true for Peter.

"I can't sleep with you anymore," he says.

In silence she listens to the explanations that follow. The whole thing with Olivia P., having to run the gauntlet at university, the hatred, the vulgarity, all of it deeply upset him, and when he came home, battered, she mocked him and something inside him broke.

He sighs. "I needed you then. For weeks I felt like a stranger in my own apartment, with my own wife. And the desire . . . it just dried up."

"What now?" she asks softly. "Are we going to live together like brother and sister from now on?"

"That's one option."

"I see!"

Her voice slides up as it always does when she's worried. Peter gives her a sympathetic look. Then he stops and does that thing with his hands – letting his arms hang and wiggling his fingers uncontrollably until he realises and crosses his hands behind his back. They're out of the wood and on a farm track. They can see the house from here.

"I mean, how do you picture that?"

"I'm not picturing anything, Rahel. I'm just telling it like it is."

His tortured face scans the fields in the distance.

"You can't force it," he says eventually.

"No. Of course not. But you can try."

"But at the moment I don't want to try anything," he says flatly, then they set off again and wander the rest of the way in silence.

□

Rahel fetches a towel from the washing line and makes straight for the lake. She plunges into the water and swims a few strokes along the shore. She doesn't dare go out very far. Whenever Rahel tried to hold on to the side in swimming lessons in the second year, the teacher would push her away with a long stick, bellowing "We're going to make tireless swimmers of you all!" across the pool. Every child who had until then felt safe now started thrashing about frantically. Rahel had feared for her life in every swimming lesson. She never learned to dive from the starting block, and during her test another swimming teacher just knocked her legs out from under her, so although she flopped in headfirst, it was a long way off a proper dive.

Now Rahel swims slowly along the thick-stemmed yellow waterlilies. She thinks of the last thing Peter said. *But at the moment I don't want to try anything.* That might mean he'll try later. He has to try. Otherwise she can't stay with him.

What is he thinking? That she'll just put up with things as they are?

She flips onto her back and allows herself to drift.

Of course there were times when she was listless and tired too. When the children were small. When they were ill, or just hard work. When Edith died. Peter never complained, never pressured her. But – and this is the crucial difference – he could always be sure that the lull would pass.

Only her face is out of the water. Her legs have sunk and something has touched them. She begins to swim rapidly.

She can now hear music coming from the other side of the lake. The teenagers from the village are gathering. Time for Rahel to go.

Wednesday

"Selma called," Peter says as he comes into the kitchen in his dressing gown. "She's asking whether she can come with the children for a few days." He wanders over to the kettle, pours the old water down the sink, fills it from the tap and adds that he's sure Ruth wouldn't mind.

Ruth wouldn't, Rahel thinks, saying nothing.

"You don't seem thrilled," he says. "You know she senses that."

Of course Rahel does. She is the psychologist in the family, after all. If only Selma weren't the way she is. It doesn't matter how much attention and love she gives her daughter – Selma needs more. During her childhood and adolescence scarcely a week went by without some existential drama. If Selma was ill, she had *hellish* pains. If Selma was heartbroken, suicide seemed *the only way out*. If there was trouble with her teachers, Selma was the *only* person that *nobody* understood, who was unfairly treated by *everyone*. The résumé of her life read: *It's all about me!*

Rahel often has to deal with people like that in her practice. People who can't put what's happened to them into perspective. Who take it all personally and are forever talking in superlatives. The *most dreadful* things happen to them, the *worst* setbacks, the *most terrible* disappointments and the *most*

39

awful betrayal. In the best cases Rahel is able to help bring about a lasting change in perspective. The truth is, such success is rare, and as far as Selma is concerned the results are crushing.

No, she didn't fall into a hole when Selma moved out. She didn't feel any emptiness or regret. She described the moment their front door closed behind Selma to Peter as a release, the end of a battle. Of course she knew that it wasn't really the end, just a ceasefire.

"I don't think that's a good idea," she now ventures, adding that the inevitable conflict with Selma might exacerbate her own difficulties. Peter blinks a few times and focuses silently on his tea ritual.

He always used to know immediately when there'd been a clash between Rahel and Selma. The state of their apartment said it all. Rahel's only way out of her inner turmoil was by establishing an external order. After the most serious incidents the fittings in the bathroom would shine and they could have eaten off the floor in the kitchen. The first time Selma cut her forearms with a razorblade, Rahel cleaned all fourteen windows including the sills inside and out.

Peter came home, looked around and said, "What happened?"

The first time Selma threatened to kill herself, Rahel took all the crockery out of the cupboard, emptied the fridge and all food cupboards, and cleaned every last nook and cranny with boiling water.

To cap it all, Selma's love life began at the tender age of fourteen. Her victims were all of a sort. Either they were unattainable older boys or boys who endlessly admired her and who she endlessly exploited. Her noisy manner, her wild, long hair, the cherry-red lipstick were a ridiculous contrast to the pallid appearance of these boys against whose backdrop she shone even more brightly. Of course she quickly got bored and dumped them the moment she began to despise them for their servility.

"Come on," Peter says. "She could do with a bit of country air." He watches over his tea like a hawk; it mustn't over-brew. "She *is* our daughter," he adds superfluously, taking the infuser out of the pot and putting it on a small plate.

"But not until Friday," she says. "And only for the weekend."

He nods. "I'll give her a bell."

Then he takes his teacup out to the yard, where the stork sticks to his heels.

□

Rahel turns on the radio and sits at the table. On the news is an item about climate change. The polar ice caps are melting, the permafrost is thawing, mountain glaciers are turning into lakes and fires are destroying huge areas of forest. Immediately she switches it off. She can take information like this only in small doses, and only when Peter is beside her. One of the last lucid things her mother said comes to mind.

"Not a bad time to die," she remarked after a similar news report. Soon afterwards she did in fact die, her flighty, bold, frivolous and neglectful mother who had such a thirst for life. When the celebrant asked about Edith's character, about the common thread that ran through her life, Rahel didn't need to think about it hard. *Not quite* were the words that best described her mother. She'd been not quite a dancer, not quite an actress, not quite a wife and, apart from the fact of two births, not quite a mother either.

She lets out a brief, solitary laugh at the idea that she's drawn a line from the vanishing polar ice caps to her mother.

"Ultimately you always end up with your mother," she says out loud, and wonders whether Selma thinks the same. Just two more days before her daughter pitches up here with great fanfare. Just two more days' peace. Rahel quickly finishes her coffee and hurries up to her room.

□

She rolls out her yoga mat for the first time since she's got here. It hasn't been used in so long that it rolls up again of its own accord. Rahel weighs down the ends with small dumb-bells she's brought along to counter the inevitable muscle wasting. She's aware that she's been lucky with her genes. So many women come to her practice who are younger than her but not as well preserved.

Rahel begins the sun salutation with arms stretched upwards and a deep breath. Then the opposite movement: the palms of her hands on the floor by her feet. She doesn't find the stretching hard. She gets her flexibility and gracefulness from her mother. Tamara takes after her father, a tall, angular man with stiff movements. Moving into the cobra, Rahel feels free and open, as the exercise promises. Her father was a handsome man, according to Edith. He was a student who disappeared after a one-night stand. She only knew his first name and never saw him again, despite searching high and low. In the downward dog the soles of her feet are fully in contact with the mat. The intense extension of her muscles is something she enjoys. After repeating the cycle fifteen times, following it with a few press-ups and twenty sit-ups, she feels full of beans.

She showers and then lies on her bed. The window is open, summer is breezing in. If the door opened now and Peter lay down beside her she'd be happy.

Not a word. Nothing all afternoon. He reads, goes for a walk with the horse, feeds the stork and strokes the cat.

At supper he lays slices of salami on bread so they don't hang over the edge. He cuts cucumber into slices of the exact same thickness, and the carrots are cut lengthwise, halved again, then neatly arranged beside the cucumber slices.

A mouthful of bread, a slice of cucumber, a baton of carrot. Bread, cucumber, carrot. Bread, cucumber, carrot.

Rahel takes a bite of a whole carrot and is anxious about the evening ahead.

"Shall we watch a film later?" she says as neutrally as possible.

Peter carefully chews his mouthful, swallows and clears his throat.

"Sure, if you like."

"What would *you* like?"

His eyes look past her and become empty. The helplessness in them makes her angry.

"A film would be good," he says suddenly, nodding a few times as if trying to convince himself of the truth of what he's said. "We haven't watched one in ages," he adds a few seconds later. Then a smile appears on his lips and he goes on eating.

Thursday

It's already midday when she sees Peter for the first time. He's been on a long walk with Baila, but doesn't look refreshed in the least. There are bags beneath his eyes.

He sleeps badly after film evenings, and he slept particularly badly last night.

He chose Lars von Trier's *Melancholia*. At a castle people are celebrating a wedding that ends in a drama, while an errant planet passes threateningly close to the earth. When it speeds on its way, the danger seems to have been dispelled, but then it turns, heading straight for the earth. The collision cannot be prevented, and only the depressive Justine – the bride – is serene about the impending end of the world. The film concludes with the planet Melancholia hitting the earth, destroying it. Peter kept staring at the screen for minutes afterwards. The credits were finished by the time he snapped out of his torpor.

"I know that feeling. I know it so well," he said quietly.

Rahel lay awake in her bed for a while, wondering what feeling he was talking about. Then she fell asleep, but woke bolt upright at three in the morning with a sudden realisation. Her heart was racing and her back was bathed in sweat. She switched on the bedside light and reached for the water bottle on the floor. Peter wasn't talking about the final scene. The feeling he claimed to know so well was depression.

□

"Did you sleep badly too?" she asks.

He nods and stops when he's beside her.

"Must've been the red wine," he says, looking at the car. "I was thinking of going shopping. Would you write me a list?"

Rahel groans. The eating habits of Selma and the children turn a simple shopping list into an impossible task, like a complex equation with a number of variables.

Even the thought of it makes her tired.

But there's no way she can send Peter off without a list.

"Best if I come too," she says, nipping into the house to fetch her bag.

When she returns he's still standing in the same spot. There's something hiding behind his smile and it occurs to Rahel that, particularly in a marriage, the sum of what isn't said far outweighs the sum of what is.

Peter suppresses a yawn. The whites of his eyes are streaked by fine red lines. "I could actually stay here," he says.

Rahel doesn't let her disappointment show. She nods, gets into the car and drives off. In the rear-view mirror she sees him standing there. He briefly raises his hand, then heads for the front door.

□

Three hours later she's back. She took her time, had an ice-cream in town, sat in the sun with a coffee and did a bit of browsing in the bookshop. For the first time in ages she bought the weekend paper she used to love reading. Until a couple of years ago, Peter would come back from the bakery at the weekend with two or three of the national papers, and while they had their breakfast they looked forward to reading them together. She can't say for sure when the unease began, but more and more often what they were reading didn't correspond with their own experience. Too many articles lacked journalistic ethos and a sense of reality, too many left them feeling they'd merely consumed a stance, a fiction, wishful thinking; and one Saturday Peter came back from the bakery with just a bag of rolls.

Rahel goes around the car and opens the boot. Peter is nowhere to be seen and when she calls out there's no reply. One of the cats trots past with a mouse in its jaws, but otherwise everything's quiet. There's nothing for it. In thirty-degree heat she can't leave the food in the car.

When she's done she hears footsteps in the corridor. He pokes his head around the door, apologises for not helping her, then goes upstairs, leaving her alone with her longing.

Rahel loads a tray with enough food and a bottle of water, takes it all up to her room and spends the rest of the day without him. She reads the novel by Elizabeth Strout in one go, and at midnight falls into an agreeable deep sleep.

Friday

Rainclouds over the woods.

Rahel gazes out of the window and disentangles her hair with her fingers. It would have to be today. The thought of being stuck inside the house with Selma and the children because of the weather does not please her. *Bring waterproofs for the boys!* she texts quickly, but Selma is probably already on her way to the station. Even the idea of all of them having lunch together is giving her a headache. To keep everyone happy she'd have to make four different meals – one for Peter and her, one for Selma and one each for Theodor and Maximilian.

Those threats and rebukes the older generation used to come out with – *You'd have starved during the war. You'll eat what you're given* – sometimes they're on the tip of Rahel's tongue.

But Selma and the children grew up without shortages. What could she and Peter have done? Fake rationing to teach them a lesson about the value of things?

In the kitchen she's standing at the open fridge, running through the options. The only vegetable they all like is broccoli. *Little trees* is what Selma used to call it when she was a girl, and the green florets pass muster with her boys too. As far as she knows there's no objection to rice either, so long as it's not

47

wholegrain. That's lunch sorted then, and when Peter comes in – in excellent spirits after his daily swim – she decides to try as hard she can to make this weekend pass peacefully.

◻

At around eleven Peter sets off for the station. He winds down the passenger window and plays "Über den Wolken" at full blast.

A wave of love surges in Rahel. Only she knows that Peter always sings along to the song quietly, from the first line – *North-easterly wind, runway zero three, I can hear the engines from here . . .* – and that he gets goosebumps every time he hears the chorus.

She stands in the yard watching the car drive away. Next to her is the stork, who seems to be missing Peter already. And then, at almost the same time as the rain, the tears come. They come so unexpectedly that Rahel gives a curt laugh before the dam breaks. Sobbing loudly she drags herself back into the house and gives free rein to her despair.

◻

By the time Selma and the children get out of the car the sun is out again, shining with the same intensity as before.

Rahel strolls over to them. Eliminating the traces of her minor breakdown wasn't easy, but the cold compresses she found in the fridge reduced the swelling around her eyes and expensive make-up did the rest.

Peter is greeted by the stork wildly flapping its wings, and when the reddish-brown cat demands attention too, the bird snaps at her.

"The animals are squabbling over your father's affection," Rahel says to Selma before they embrace briefly. Theo and Max wait beside the car, each holding a stick. They stare spellbound at the stork, then run over to it and look surprised when the bird makes itself scarce.

"You gave him a fright," Selma tells them. "If you approach him slowly he might not run off."

But their sturdy bodies are on the move again, this time in pursuit of the fleeing cat. Smiling, Selma shakes her head.

"Boys," she remarks soberly.

And she looks surprisingly good. Motherhood of two small children hasn't left any traces. Selma's lipstick glistens cherry-red as ever and she's carefully applied mascara to her lashes, which are thick anyway. She's a beautiful young mother.

For a moment Rahel is ashamed. Her worries about the weekend suddenly seem unfounded and – what's worse – she feels heartless. Selma looks around, then takes her phone out of her bag and grimaces.

"Shit! No reception! Fucking cheapo network!"

Rahel shrugs. "It might work if you stand on the big boulder on the drive. Otherwise you can borrow mine."

Selma nods. "Would you keep an eye on the kids for a moment?" she asks, heading off without waiting for an answer.

□

When Selma returns, Rahel has already set the table and is slicing fruit for pudding. The boys help themselves without asking.

"Wash your hands first!" she calls out, putting a stool in front of the sink. They don't even look up; they just stuff their mouths with slices of apple, chunks of banana, apricots and raspberries, all at once, then snort with laughter. Pulped fruit

49

is running down their chins. Theo pulls up his T-shirt and wipes it off. Max copies him.

Selma sits on the chair by the window, lays her phone on the windowsill and asks, "Why don't you own your own house? Or at least an apartment?"

Just in time Peter comes through the door. He grins and pinches a few pieces of fruit with feigned greediness. Theo protests vociferously. "Because we're Easterners," Peter mumbles, seemingly unaffected by his daughter's insolence. "Nobody taught us you had to strive for property. Nobody taught us that you're better off letting money work for you rather than working yourself. I'm afraid, Selma, that your mother and I grasped the basic rules of capitalism far too late."

Rahel casts him a look of gratitude. She tears off a few pieces of kitchen roll, wipes the boys' sticky hands and herds them to the sink.

"Leave them," Selma says.

Rahel groans. "Do you want them getting stung by wasps later?"

Despite their protests she wipes the boys' faces with a cloth.

"Anyway . . ." Selma continues, ". . . my friends in the West are all inheriting something."

"I'm only forty-nine," Rahel says sweetly. "If you're unlucky I'll be around for another forty years."

"I didn't mean it like that, Mum."

"You and Simon will inherit something too," Peter chips in. "A bit of money and a bookshelf full of valuable first editions. And, best of all, you'll get the chance to do everything better than us."

Selma silently winds a strand of hair around her right

forefinger. Rahel says nothing. One thing's for certain: if Vincent weren't so selfless and hardworking, Selma would sink into poverty. After two semesters studying Language, Literature and Culture she took a break because Theodor was on the way, and when Theo was eighteen months old and Selma ready to resume, she became pregnant with Max.

"How's Vincent?" Rahel says innocently, looking her daughter in the eye.

"Fine, fine . . . Yup, fine."

An answer that makes even Peter sit up and listen. She can see it in his slightly cocked head and rapid blinking.

Vincent is a godsend for Selma. Everybody knows that; it's only Selma who takes him and the sacrifices he makes for their young family for granted. She met him playing volleyball. Vince immediately fell for the cheeky girl in her skimpy bikini. After studying Business Informatics in almost record time he began as a trainee at the Sächsische Aufbaubank. In Selma's nineteen-year-old eyes he was a real man and when, just a few weeks after they met, she announced she wanted to marry him, Rahel was initially speechless, then relieved. Vince was like an invisible net stopping a bouncy rubber ball from drifting off. At a stroke, those times of Rahel lying awake all night because of Selma were over.

Now he's climbed a fair way up the career ladder at SAB. Rahel can't remember the exact job title, nor can Selma. But it's to do with data and security, she knows that much.

As far as a potential inheritance is concerned, they can expect substantially less from Vincent's family. When Rahel first asked about his parents, Selma replied, "Victims of reunification." In the same unsympathetic tone, she added, "The usual: company folded, no more job, missed the boat, illness, depression, etc."

"Why didn't Vincent come?" Rahel now probes.

Selma pokes around her plate and mutters something about work and stress. Then she starts eating rapidly, glancing regularly at her mobile. Theo slides off the chair they've raised with a cushion and sits beneath the table. Rahel looks on in horror as Selma passes him his plate.

"He likes eating under the table at the moment. I've read that it's a normal phase. You mustn't interfere, they say, or it might affect the child's development."

"I see," is the only thing Rahel can come out with.

Max, who they've bundled into an old child's seat, is behaving like a savage. He wants to go under the table too. Before the chair breaks from his writhing, Peter pulls the boy out and puts him on the floor beside his brother.

"Please don't expect us to understand," he says to Selma.

Selma clears her throat.

"If you force children to do things at mealtimes," she explains with deliberate slowness, "they can develop eating disorders."

"Then almost everyone in my generation would have an eating disorder," Peter replies kindly and calmly, then adds, "I don't think that's the case."

Selma lets go of her cutlery.

"Are you being serious, Dad? Are you doubting me yet again?"

"He's not doubting *you*, Selma," Rahel says energetically, "but the assumption that children who are made to sit at the table develop eating disorders. You, by the way, were only allowed to eat at the table."

"Don't try to tell me that didn't harm me, Mum," Selma snaps. "You've no idea what my therapist—"

"Your *therapist*?"

"Oh yes. I've started psychoanalysis. It's going to take three years but I think it'll be worth it."

"Psychoanalysis?" Rahel echoes. At that moment something tepid and damp lands on her right foot.

"Ugh!" she squeals, yanking her foot back. With a sigh, Peter puts his cutlery down in an "A" I'm-still-eating shape, as if there were a waiter around who'd clear the plate away otherwise.

"There are limits," he says wearily. In turn he pulls the boys out from beneath the table, sets them back in their seats and says to them rather unconvincingly "That's enough!"

While Rahel picks the chewed-up broccoli off her foot, a film plays in her mind. She knows exactly what Selma will bring out in her two to three hundred hours of therapy, and as Selma still goes by her maiden name, it won't be hard for the analyst to put two and two together. Forget patient confidentiality, sooner or later at some meeting with other therapists it will come out that the psychologist and psychotherapist Rahel Wunderlich totally fucked up her daughter. Oh, sometimes they're on the tip of her tongue, all those unnecessary and wrongheaded phrases:

How can you do this to me? Why are you so ungrateful? Haven't I done everything for you?

But it would only make everything worse, and besides, she'd be lying.

When Peter picks up his cutlery again, and even Theo and Max are eating with a hint of table manners, Rahel looks her daughter in the eye and thinks how they took her away when she was six weeks old, in their first Western car, an old Renault 5. One morning they set out from Dresden and headed east to Sebnitz, on the edge of Saxon Switzerland. There, Peter's mother took the little bundle in her arms and carried her into the house where everything was ready. There was a cot in the spare room, powdered formula and baby bottles in the kitchen, and improvised changing facilities on top of the washing machine in the bathroom. To begin with Peter and Rahel would take their baby home at weekends, but after a while, especially when exams were looming, they prolonged the gaps between visits, sometimes going to Sebnitz only once a month. Peter's mother described Selma as an uncomplicated, bouncy baby who was always laughing. When, years later, Rahel learned on a course that this behaviour was typical of infants of depressive mothers or babies severely emotionally neglected for other reasons, she burst into tears. Peter's mother had battled with depression for many years. At the time, giving her the baby to look after seemed the best solution. Peter and she could study in peace, Peter's mother got something meaningful to do and Selma was being cared for by her own family.

"Why are you staring at me like that?" Selma frowns. "It's creepy."

"Sorry," Rahel mumbles, turning back to her food. If only you knew, she thinks, and it strikes her that she will know soon. Analysts begin with the primordial soup; in Selma's case this means infantile attachment disorder.

Does Selma realise the full significance of this? Till now she hasn't made much of her early separation from her parents. Once, when Theo was six weeks old, exactly the age Selma had been, she asked, "How could you give such a little baby away?" Her gaze was fixed on Theo, sleeping peacefully in her lap. Then, after a brooding pause: "Didn't it break your heart?"

This second question excluded Peter. In Selma's view, only the mother's heart could be broken. Rahel said something like *It was hard, but there was no other choice*, and astonishingly Selma accepted this answer straightaway. Totally understandable from a professional perspective. *My mother didn't have a choice* was less painful than *She took the easier option and sacrificed me*.

No doubt Selma will soon throw all this at her.

◻

After lunch Peter and she leave the battlefield in the kitchen and have coffee on the bench beside the front door. The boys' voices screech at them from one of the upstairs windows. Before Selma moved into the room with them, Rahel pointed out to her gently that this wasn't their house and most of the things in it were old. Selma groaned but didn't protest – a sign that she understood the reason for Rahel's caution.

Peter is sitting a good metre away from her. He strokes the one-eared cat that knocks his trouser leg with her tail in a monotonous rhythm. The cat purrs so loudly she almost sounds threatening. This charmless animal has his undivided attention. In the past after a meal like that they would have smiled at each other surreptitiously, and this knowing smile would have emphasised their unity. Today Peter is utterly content to have an old nag, a damaged cat and a needy stork for company.

Upstairs the racket subsides and Selma's voice rings out. She's singing her boys a song, and singing it so beautifully that Peter stops stroking the cat and lifts his head. Rahel tries to catch his eye and earns a smile.

"She's taking singing lessons," he tells her. "She told me on the way here."

Over the years, the list of activities Selma has begun with passion is long. In most cases the enthusiasm would flatten out after four to six weeks, and after three months at most Rahel would write to say her daughter was stopping the music, dance or sports lessons. As far as she can remember, singing has not yet featured on the list.

Rahel holds her face towards the sun. She squints a little and sees a bird of prey circling in the cloudless sky. It's quiet in the children's room. Now Peter will get up and retire for an afternoon nap. She hears the words before he says them, then he does actually say them and goes inside.

This is the moment for the cigarette. She hurries into the kitchen with her empty cup to make a second coffee, but finds Peter standing there.

"I thought you were going to have a lie-down," she says. It almost sounds reproachful.

He points at the overflowing sink. "I can hardly leave you alone with all this chaos."

Together they tidy up the kitchen. Their tasks are clearly allocated; they don't get in each other's way. When eventually Peter leaves and fresh coffee steams in Rahel's cup, she hears footsteps approaching along the corridor.

"Right, they're asleep at last," Selma says, sitting down. "Do I get one?" she asks, nodding at Rahel's coffee.

Rahel turns away and opens the cupboard. For an exaggeratedly long time she looks for a suitable cup, all the while keeping a check on her expression, which she wants to be neither happy nor irritated, then turns to her daughter with as neutral a face as she can manage.

"Everything alright?" Selma asks. "You look sort of stressed."

"Everything's great," Rahel says, sitting beside her and pouring some coffee.

"I'd totally forgotten how beautiful it is here," Selma says. "It's paradise for the children."

"It must be," Rahel says, sighing.

"I'm the only one of our friends who can never say: *We're taking the children to their grandparents' in the country*," Selma complains.

"It's always about you," Rahel says, taking a large gulp.

"Huh?"

"That's your perception, my darling," she explains. "You're always the *only one* who something happens to or doesn't happen to."

"But it's true!"

"And now you're here. In the country. With the grandparents."

"But it's not your house."

"There's always something," Rahel replies with great composure.

Selma leans back so violently that the chair almost topples over.

"There's no point," she hisses. "It's just impossible to talk to you."

"Do you also have a go at Vincent's parents for not having a country house?"

Selma laughs hysterically.

"Vincent's dad has taken ear-ly re-tire-ment. And his mother works on the till at a phar-ma-cy."

"And?" Rahel plays dumb.

"How are they supposed to buy a house? You, on the other hand. Dad's a professor and you've got your own practice. I bet people like you in the West at least own their apartment."

Rahel wishes Peter were here to give this angry young woman the right answers.

An image flashes in her mind: tiny Selma lying screaming in her cot. But nobody comes to comfort her. And she remembers the proud reports from Peter's mother: at six months Selma slept through the night, at eighteen months she was out of nappies in the daytime, and she was always laughing. Such a friendly child, the neighbours said, a ray of sunshine.

"I'm popping into the studio," Rahel tells Selma, who's started scratching her head. It's what she always does when she's nervous, angry or bored, and Rahel carried out endless unnecessary lice treatments because of it. With a sigh she gets up and leaves the kitchen.

□

Outside she's met by silence. She closes the door behind her and makes straight for the workbench where the cigarette must be somewhere behind the books. Dust dances in a broad shaft of sunlight, and a fat bluebottle keeps crashing into the windowpane. She catches sight of the note: *Pray without ceasing!*

What made him write this? Does it inspire him? Does he think praying is necessary for some reason?

She's glad to have her thoughts diverted from Selma to Viktor. She can picture him vividly, albeit not as he looks today. When she thinks of Viktor, she always remembers a man of about forty, in the prime of his life – tall, muscular, badly shaven, with shining blue, friendly eyes and longish hair tied at the nape of his neck.

He was a member of the East German Association of Artists. He won prizes and was occasionally allowed to travel to non-communist countries for study purposes. Before the Wall came down he visited the Louvre in Paris. She remembers this because he brought her back a gift: a poster of the Nike of Samothrace. At the time she didn't know what to do with it, but later she framed it and hung it in the kitchen of her first apartment.

Viktor was always working, and thanks to his membership of the Association of Artists he was never – unlike those who voiced their opposition to the regime – short of materials or tools. Edith and Ruth once had an argument about it. Edith had called Viktor a *state artist*, and Ruth, ever controlled, lost her composure for a moment and used harsh words with Edith and her current lover, an artist too but clearly less in favour with the state.

In the early 1990s Viktor suffered a serious crisis. Because money was short he took on private commissions and made sculptures for the gardens of nouveau-riche houseowners. Small copies of the Venus de Milo or Michelangelo's David were popular, and his consumption of alcohol and cigarettes, which till then had been moderate, became alarming. Clients were not interested in his own designs; they found them too bulky, too abstract, not pleasing enough. But he and Ruth had to live off something.

Ruth had lost her job shortly after reunification when the cultural centre of the region's major town where she'd given ballet lessons, which had been run by a combine, had to close, as did the combine.

For Viktor it was more than a decade before the tide turned. In the noughties people suddenly seemed to remember him, inviting him to exhibitions, writing articles about him, and a Berlin gallery owner drove out to his country home with a draft contract. He became famous at a stroke, practically overnight.

At last Rahel has the cigarette between her fingers. She twists her hand back and forth and reaches for the lighter.

"What's that, Mum? A stress ciggie?"

Selma is standing in the doorway. A warm breeze brushes

Rahel's arms. She sees one of the cats scurry past Selma and disappear behind a large Ruth sculpture.

"Oh no, the cat!" she says. "How are we going to get it out?"

"Leave the door open," Selma says, wandering in.

Rahel puts down the cigarette and lighter.

"It must be amazing to create something like that from nothing," Selma says after taking a look around. She touches an unfinished wooden sculpture on one of the tables. Then she turns abruptly to Rahel. "There's nothing I can do really well," she says, and a few seconds later adds, "Apart from drawing, perhaps."

From the corner of her eye Rahel sees the cat race past. Towards the door, thank God.

"Oh yes, you were always good at drawing," Rahel confirms. "And you've got a lovely voice. Apart from that you're . . . a loving mother."

She says these last words softly, almost in a whisper. When she sees the brief flash in her daughter's eyes she wants to hug Selma and beg her forgiveness. But what then? The Pandora's Box would be open, Selma would start to feel sorry for herself and nobody would be better off.

Rahel takes a step towards Selma and gazes at the sculpture.

"Out of root wood," Selma says.

Rahel nods and refrains from correcting her. It's burr, which most people mistakenly call root wood. Looking more closely, Rahel makes out the form of a curled-up cat. The surface is smooth and dark and has an incredibly beautiful structure. Only the head of the cat looks unfinished. Selma runs her fingers over it.

"Look, it's the one-eared cat! It would be a fantastic birthday present for Dad. Could you ask Viktor if we can buy it?"

"I don't know if Viktor's head is in the right place for that sort of thing at the moment. I don't even know if he's able to understand anything, or speak."

Rahel swallows. Her imagination resolutely dismisses the image of an old and decrepit stroke patient. *His sharp intellect concludes, no: what mustn't be true cannot be so*, Peter would say now, in the process demonstrating his limitless recall of quotations.

"Selma?" Peter is calling. Then he's in the doorway, carrying Theo.

"Oh, my little mouse!" Selma says, taking Theo from Peter's arms.

"Max is still asleep."

Peter's hair is all over the place and his shirt wrongly buttoned up. Theo must have woken him from his afternoon sleep. For a moment Theo snuggles into his mother and sticks his thumb in his mouth. But a few seconds later he's already pushing away, keen to get down. The little rascal in Viktor's sanctum – that's too much for Rahel's nerves. Before he can get up to any mischief she shoos him gently outside. Selma follows, her disapproval of the eviction writ large on her face.

□

Until supper they go their own ways. Peter is off with Baila and Theo, and Selma and Max have made their way down to the swimming spot.

Rahel is working in the garden. The rain has perked everything up. She goes around with secateurs and a receptacle for weeds, dead-heading and pruning the shrubs, removing yellow leaves from the rhododendron, laying manure around the hydrangeas and roses, and taking a handful of lavender

61

flowers to her room, where she wraps them in a handkerchief and puts them amongst her clothes. Yesterday she saw a moth fly across the room.

She's about to put lavender in Peter's room too, but then she hears the phone ring downstairs.

It's Ruth. She enquires briefly about the animals, asks how she and Peter are, meets the news about Selma's arrival with a brusque "Yes, yes, no problem", then comes straight onto Viktor.

"He's not the same," she says, and there's a long pause. Rahel listens so intently to the silence that for a moment she forgets to breathe. Ruth then tells her that Viktor is able to walk, but only slowly and haltingly; he's able to talk, but only in short sentences; and he's able to eat, but just forgets to. She's fully aware of his condition; his days as a working artist are over. His fine motor skills are shot, making it impossible for him to use tools again. Although the neurologist and the physiotherapist have been making hopeful noises, the long timescale they've mentioned has disheartened him.

"That man is my life, Rahel," Ruth says softly. "But he's just . . . no longer . . . the same."

She is silent again and Rahel fancies she can hear a stifled sob, but when Ruth says goodbye her voice sounds as steady and determined as ever.

She feels more for combative individuals than maudlin ones. Something that Selma learned in the course of her gruelling puberty.

"It's strange that you should have chosen to become a psychologist," she said, throwing a handful of crisps into her mouth before adding, "I mean, you only like winners. You've no time for weaklings."

Rahel didn't defend herself, even though it wasn't true.

62

The victory wasn't important to her; what she respected was the battle.

She goes out to the yard and sees Peter approaching with Baila. Theo is sitting proudly on the horse, holding on tight to its mane. An energetic "Brrr!" makes the mare stop and Theo drops from the horse's back straight into Peter's arms.

"We got as far as trotting!" Peter tells her. "The boy is absolutely fearless."

He laughs, shaking his head, and takes Baila to the stable.

Selma comes around the corner too, with Max singing on her shoulders. She squats to let him down and immediately has Theo in her arms. No wonder she's always so exhausted and edgy. The children stick to her. They hang off her back, sit on her shoulders or demand to be carried. Even though both have been able to walk for ages.

Rahel never had this kind of closeness with either Selma or Simon. She could have done, but at the time nobody dragged their children around like that. They would lie in prams or bassinets, and later stand in a playpen until they could walk. This was the early nineties when in the East there were more important things to do than carry babies around. They should be happy they were born at all! The dip in the birth rate after the collapse of the GDR was dramatic. Of Rahel's former classmates many had only one child and some had none at all.

☐

Supper passes astonishingly peacefully. Theo stuffs bits of bread with *Leberwurst* into his mouth one after another and chews with relish. Now and then Selma posts a bit of cucumber or apple in between. Max, who for good reason is wearing a bib with sleeves, is spooning in semolina with apple sauce.

When Peter offers Selma another glass of wine she puts a hand over her glass.

"You know you two are alcoholics!" she says in a friendly but haughty tone that elicits a laugh from Rahel.

"I wouldn't laugh if I was you," Selma says.

"*Were* you," Rahel corrects her.

Then they go on eating as if nothing had happened, and Peter talks again of his excursion with Baila and Theo, going into every detail about Baila's fear of raised hunting hides, flapping tarpaulin, wood stacks and birds taking flight. Every time the mare did a little leap to the side, her ears back, and Theo laughed and called out, "Oops!"

When he hears his grandfather talking about him he smiles impishly and repeats "Oops!" a few times.

At around eight o'clock Selma takes the children to bed. She seems to have fallen asleep with them; at any rate she doesn't come back down. Peter retires to his room too. Rahel waits till ten, then goes upstairs a little disappointed and a little relieved.

She never knows which way a conversation with Selma will turn, and tomorrow is another day.

Saturday

It's rained again overnight and when Rahel opens her window in the morning a fresh, cool breeze blows in from the woods.

She slept with earplugs because of the children. This way of plugging yourself off from the world was one of Peter's recommendations. He's been using them every night for years. She too has come to appreciate peace and quiet. After almost two decades of bringing up children, it feels good only to be listening inwards, as if wrapped in cotton wool, and no longer having to be on call at night. Selma is responsible for Max and Theo's nocturnal antics.

Yesterday passed so peacefully that Rahel is looking forward to today. She unrolls her yoga mat and stretches. Outside she hears the call of a buzzard and the clacking of hoofs in the cobbled yard. Peter is taking Baila to the paddock. His sympathy for the mare is growing by the day. "A herd animal without a herd," he said yesterday with a shake of the head. "If only there were another horse here."

"But she's got you," Rahel replied with a grin, earning a meaningful look.

The clacking of hooves fades and the buzzard is quiet now too. But she can hear the boys' voices in the yard.

"Come on, let's see if the chickens have laid any eggs,"

Selma calls out cheerily, and they immediately run off, whooping.

Rahel is alone in the house. Standing on the mat with her feet apart, she stretches her arms upwards, breathes in and begins the familiar cycle of movements. She repeats the sun salutation ten times, then feels uplifted and ready to face the day.

In the kitchen she finds Peter, who briefly strokes her arm as he passes. She can still feel his touch minutes later, and when they sit opposite each other at the table the space between them seems to have contracted. Then the door opens and the boys burst into the gentle atmosphere of the morning.

❑

After breakfast Rahel gets to work on another of the neglected flowerbeds while the rest of the family head off for the lake.

"I might go to the grocery," Rahel calls after them. Selma turns and calls back, "Grocery? Stop talking like you're still in the GDR. It's called a su-per-mar-ket these days!"

Rahel spends a good hour tending the flowerbed. Afterwards she kneels in front of it and surveys the results. She lays her hands on the soft, damp soil, digs in her fingers and stays like that for a while; in her mind she's drawing energy from the earth like a plant. She smiles at how she must look, but nobody can see her, she's not bothering anybody. Then – on the spur of the moment – she gets up, washes her hands in one of the water butts and goes into the studio.

❑

Rahel looks at the drawings, one after the other. She waits for them to speak to her. The one depicting her as a child causes a sharp pain inside. The young girl's face bears an expression of maturity before its time. Viktor has portrayed a despondency she can vividly recall.

Her mother could have saved her from this. Rahel shouldn't have allowed Edith just to slip away. If Ruth hadn't been there the whole time, if she hadn't sat beside the dying woman's bed as if glued to it, Rahel might have summoned the courage to insist one last time. She never really bought her mother's line that it would be pointless trying to look for Rahel's father.

Now it's too late. With Edith's death the truth was buried too.

What if Viktor's her father? She wouldn't have put it past Edith.

Rahel returns the sheets of paper to the drawer, picks up the cigarette, twiddles it uncertainly and puts it down again. It's a monstrous thought. A lifelong lie of such magnitude. She supports herself on the drawing cabinet with both hands, then storms across the yard into the house and upstairs to her room. Frantically she searches for her phone and calls Tamara.

"Hi Tamara," Rahel says, then comes straight out with it. "I'm going to ask you something and I want you to tell me the truth. It's really—"

"Thanks for asking, Rahel," Tamara interrupts her. "Not too bad, all things considered. Bernd, could you make sure the rice doesn't burn? I'm on the phone to my sister. Right, I'm back."

"Tamara, please!"

"Alright, what do you want to know?"

"Did Mum ever talk to you about my father? Do you know who he is?"

"What? Do you think I'd have kept that from you?"

67

Rahel takes a deep breath. "I don't know. That's why I'm asking."

"Typical. You always think the worst of me. Apparently I always used to be envious of you and your husband and your wonderful children, and now I'm a liar too."

"I didn't say that."

"But that's what it boils down to, Rahel."

Then, after a pause and in a weary voice, "Rahel, I've no idea who your father is. Mum never spoke to me about it. And right now I've got bigger problems to deal with. Bernd's eyes are getting worse. His field of vision is becoming more and more restricted. In a year or two he'll be blind. Our son can barely scrape together his rent, a trade fair contractor with no trade fairs . . . Well, the pandemic has hit some harder than others. That's our life at the moment, Rahel. Soon I'm going to be the only one here earning."

"I'm sorry, Tamara. I'm really sorry."

"Oh well, that's life. Look, I've got to get back to the kitchen."

When Rahel puts down her mobile a wave of heat shoots through her body. The most obvious thing hadn't occurred to her: she ought to have offered to help Tamara. Immediately she starts to type a message, but before she can send it Selma comes in.

"Can I have a word, Mum?"

Without waiting for an answer she walks past her and sits on the bed.

"I might be splitting up with Vince," she says, lifting her head and crossing her arms. Then she begins to sob. It's heart-wrenching to hear. Her body is quivering and her hands are trembling. Rahel hurries to sit beside her daughter and puts her arms around her.

□

When Selma goes upstairs after lunch with the children, Peter and Rahel remain in the kitchen. He loads the dishwasher while she makes coffee. Then they go outside and sit on a bench behind the barn.

"You've got to talk her out of it," Peter implores her. "She doesn't have a *single* concrete reason . . . She says her *feelings* have changed somehow." He waves his hands in the air. "Her feelings! Changed! Please tell her that's normal. Feelings *do* change. *Our* feelings have changed too."

Rahel shoots him a suspicious look that he doesn't appear to notice.

"But they're not sleeping with each other anymore," she points out, "and she's fallen in love with someone else . . ."

"So, they don't have sex for a while. And as for falling in love with—"

"Peter! She's young. At that age it still matters."

He shakes his head

"Men are always accused of being driven by desire, but I get the feeling you women are surpassing us in that area too."

She almost laughs, but this rare display of irritability prevents her.

"Of course you call it something different," he continues. "With women it goes by the name of emancipation!"

"What's up with you all of a sudden?" Rahel shifts away from him slightly.

"Nothing. I'm just not going to stand idly by and watch our daughter destroy her family on a whim. Besides, our apartment doesn't work for that many people."

"What's that supposed to mean?"

"Oh, so she hasn't told you? To begin with she wants to

move in with the children. I mean, she doesn't have a job or any money."

There's no hesitation before Rahel says, "No!" Whatever else Peter says goes straight over her head. While he's thinking that there's something of Edith in Selma's skittishness, an image forms in Rahel's mind: their apartment plunged into chaos, Theo and Max with chocolate smeared all over their hands and mouths, she herself at the cooker and Peter taking refuge in his room. The only thing missing from this picture is Selma. "No, they can't," she hears herself say in an unfamiliar voice.

"It would be OK in an emergency," Peter says, "but this isn't an emergency. She's fallen for some dodgy bloke who does something in art."

"Electroacoustic installations," Rahel clarifies.

"Electroacoustic installations!" he repeats, annoyed. "The perfect job to provide for a family. Totally crisis-proof."

Rahel puts a hand on his arm, but he brushes it off.

"I'm going for a walk," he mutters, getting up and heading across the meadow towards the woods.

❑

Rahel goes back to the house in an autumnal mood. Taking a detour she sees Selma from a distance standing on the boulder. With her mobile to her ear she sways perilously, gesticulating with her free arm and jerking her head back. Struck by a sudden lethargy, Rahel slinks past and comes across a bizarre sight: the stork loping across the yard, flanked by four cats. It seems to have grown in confidence over the past few days; now it brazenly makes for the front door and flaps its wings wildly at the threshold. The cats hiss and scatter, and Rahel hears Baila whinny in the distance. What's going on? An uprising? Rahel creeps up and says, "Shoo! Shoo!" to get rid of Mr Stork. It's now so hot that she just wants to get inside. "Shoo! Shoo!" she says again, but the bird won't budge. She takes the broom leaning against the wall and sweeps in his direction. Eventually he trudges off, unhurriedly and rather unfazed, but the door is now free.

Once in her room she lies down on the bed. Peter's right: they will have to make Selma see sense. Rahel closes her eyes and thinks up a few smart sentences, studded with everything she's learned from her professional experience: praise, esteem and an acknowledgement of all inconsistencies. She also braces herself for the recriminations, and promises herself she'll remain calm even if the accusations are overblown.

She sees it every day in her practice. All those things that parents are supposedly to blame for! By today's standards Edith would surely have lost custody of her children. Along with half the other parents. Even stinting on praise would cause indignation nowadays. Not long ago one of her younger clients complained that her parents had only ever praised her for special achievements. *Why else?* Rahel almost asked, but thought better of it and formulated her words differently.

"I suppose praise was particularly important to you."

When all she got in reply was a shrug, Rahel probed further.

"Would you have taken your parents seriously if they'd kept praising you for obvious things? Would praise still have been important to you then?"

The young woman began chewing her bottom lip and shrugged again. Rahel told her to take this question away and ponder it for next time. Like so many of her younger patients, this one judged everything by ideal rather than real standards. The inevitable outcome is failure.

Rahel has noticed similar tendencies in Selma. Muttering to herself she rehearses the speech she's going to give her daughter. With short, clear, friendly sentences she'll build a bridge of understanding between them. She closes her eyes, the muttering becomes a babbling, then her thoughts blur and she sinks into a shallow sleep.

□

She wakes with a start. It feels as if she's been asleep for hours, and yet only thirty minutes have passed. In front of the mirror she ties her hair up and dabs cream under her eyes.

In the kitchen Selma is sitting at the table with a vacant look. "He wants the children," she gasps before Rahel can sit down.

"Who wants the children?"

"Vincent!"

"Nice and calm, and let's take it from the beginning."

"Vince and I had an argument on the phone. I told him I didn't think we could go on anymore, and he said I could leave but the children would stay with him."

"Hang on. This isn't something you can discuss over the phone. You can't end your marriage over the phone." The image of Selma standing on the boulder, her dress wafting and the mobile at her ear, pops into her mind. Instinctively she shakes her head.

"He provoked me, and—"

"How?"

"He wanted to know if Max and Theo were going to bed too late. And if they were running around barefoot because they haven't had their tetanus injections yet . . . all that sort of stuff. He always knows better!"

Rahel doesn't reply.

"I know, I know," Selma adds caustically, "you and Dad think Vince is the best thing since sliced bread."

"We have a high regard for Vince, and that means we really respect you too. I mean, you were the one who chose him."

"But it was a mistake, Mum!"

"You've got two children – it can't have been that much of a mistake."

Rahel doesn't hear Peter coming. His face is red and there are patches of sweat on the armpits of his otherwise immaculate shirt. He grabs a glass, fills it from the tap and drinks it in one. Then he joins them at the table.

"Of course the children aren't a mistake," Selma concedes.

"Well, that's a good starting point." Peter strokes Selma's hair and for the next half hour at least she doesn't reject outright her parents' suggestions for resolving the conflict. Just before all three of them are shaken by a racket on the stairs, Rahel has even managed to get her to agree to some marriage counselling.

When she sees the children, Selma's face lights up. Max is wearing nothing apart from a suspiciously low-hanging nappy and a much too large welly on his right foot. Theo has the left boot, but is otherwise naked. He climbs nimbly onto Selma's lap. From this position of safety he makes a stern face as he fends off Max's clumsy attempts to get up too. Each time Max's little hands dig into Selma's dress, Theo forcefully pushes his brother away.

"No, Theo," Selma says softly and gives him a kiss. With a sharp intake of breath Rahel grabs Max and lifts him up.

Don't make me a grandmother too soon. I need at least ten years' break, was one of the last things she said to Selma the day their daughter left home. Not that she really believed Selma would heed these words, but she was keen to articulate them.

Max is not at all happy with this outcome.

"Maamaaa!" he whines, holding his arms out to Selma. So much strength in such a little body! Rahel holds him in a tight embrace, but still he almost manages to wriggle from her grasp.

"Maamaaa!" Theo moans, nestling closer to Selma and looking at his brother with cold curiosity. Not a hint of empathy. Selma sighs and puts Theo down.

"I'm off to the boulder again," she says, picking up her mobile and going out.

Before the children can go running after their mother, Peter closes the door and stands beside it like a sentry. Rahel promises to make the boys pancakes, which appeases them for the time being.

"Who's she calling now? Vincent or the installator?"

"Vincent is my daddy!" Theo says.

Rahel shoots Peter an acid glance and puts a finger to her lips. The boy is more observant than she thought.

"Go upstairs and get changed," she tells him. Then she assembles the ingredients for the batter and sends Peter off to the bathroom with Max to change his nappy.

Theo comes plodding back into the kitchen in just a T-shirt.

"Do you know what, Granny?" he shouts above the noise of the mixer.

"What?" Rahel shouts back.

"My daddy cried."

She switches off the mixer and turns to him. Theo rubs his eyes and pretends to sob loudly.

"And my mummy did this."

He picks up a cup from the table and throws it on the floor before Rahel can stop him. With his head cocked he looks at the shards.

"Broken," he says, then clambers onto one of the chairs where he sits up very straight.

"Grown-ups argue too, just like Max and you. But they make up again afterwards." Rahel is not especially convinced by what she's just said. She sweeps up the shards with a brush.

When the first golden pancake disappears bit by bit into Theo's mouth, she breathes a sigh of relief. It's as everyone says: little children, little worries; big children, big worries. The fact that Selma can't even pull herself together in front of the children isn't a good sign.

□

She drops the subject for the rest of the day. Peter doesn't seem interested in continuing the conversation either. The peace lasts till the evening, through supper and until bedtime. Tomorrow, Rahel thinks before turning out the light, tomorrow we'll see.

Sunday

In the middle of a sun salutation her room is invaded by Theo and Max.

"Back in a sec," Selma calls from the corridor.

The boys leap onto the mat and romp about wildly.

"Where's Opa?" Rahel asks, hoping to get rid of them.

"With the chickens," they say in unison. Then they get into a scrap and Rahel lets them have the mat with a sigh. She goes into the bathroom next door and looks in the mirror. I wouldn't gaze back at me, she thinks.

If she's unlucky she'll never be desired again. Will never be flushed with passion again. Instead, like so many ageing women, she'll throw herself into the grandchildren and find a different sort of fulfilment in looking after these young, vigorous shoots, gradually forgetting herself and her own needs. And this forgetting will ensure that over time her womanhood becomes neutralised and soon she'll be regarded only as a grandmother and no longer as a woman.

She takes a towel and puts it over her head. Then she pulls a terrible face and peers in at the children who interrupt their brawl at the sight of her and start screeching.

❑

Later they all get together in the kitchen. Selma is looking fresh, almost sunny, something that doesn't escape Peter's notice either.

"Very jolly this morning," he says.

Selma grins and shrugs, as if to say: why not? The boisterous way she's playing with the children and her healthy appetite arouse Rahel's suspicion. When the boys have finished their porridge and run outside, she asks straight out. Selma seems to have been expecting it.

"I think . . ." she declares solemnly, ". . . that I've finally worked out what I want to do as a career."

Peter raises his eyebrows and Rahel just says, "Oh?"

"You both know how much I like drawing. The other day I drew a picture story for Theo. And in Leipzig there's a course in book design and illustration—"

"In Leipzig?"

"Yes, in Leipzig!" Selma says with defiant resolve, giving Rahel a dark look. "Anyway, Leipzig's meant to be much cooler than Dresden."

"What about the children?" Rahel immediately asks.

"We'll have to see . . . I mean, I haven't thought it through fully."

"I can see that," Peter says.

Selma looks from the one to the other. She purses her lips and narrows her eyes.

"You're so . . . so . . ."

"Conventional?" Peter asks. "Boring? We're your parents, Selma, not your friends. It's not our job to tell you what you want to hear. We also have to say things you don't like."

Without another word Selma storms out of the door. Keeping up with the way her head works is impossible. Yesterday she thought marriage guidance might help, and today

– presumably after a phone call to the electroacoustic bloke –
she's intending to turn her life upside down. Burying her head
in her hands, Rahel stays sitting at the table in silence.

"Hey," Peter says, putting a hand on her shoulder. "You
know what she's like. A lot of fuss about nothing."

"I'm not so sure about that," she mumbles.

Rahel has always found it a bit much the way Selma just
comes out with the most half-baked ideas. She'd almost forgotten how hard it is for her to keep level-headed when that
happens.

Through the window she can see Selma carrying Max. He's
pressing his little hands onto his mother's cheeks and says
something that makes Selma laugh, before wriggling out of
her arms.

A shudder runs down Rahel's spine. She's forgotten that
she too could now be the mother of a small child.

Not long after her forty-fifth birthday she discovered she
was pregnant. Above all it made her angry. Angry at herself
and her carelessness. She could barely remember the sex itself, whereas other couples went to God knows what lengths
to conceive. Angry at Peter, because her body had to go
through the procedure of an abortion whereas he remained
untouched. Angry at his reaction.

When she told him he looked at her in pleasant surprise,
but she hissed, "Peter! I'm forty-five!"

And with that the matter was decided. Appointments
were made, the abortion carried out and scarcely another word
was uttered about it. They said nothing to the children, of
course.

"I'll go out and chat to her," Peter says, interrupting
her thoughts. She nods and thinks that people who don't
have children somehow remain children themselves. They

may be great people, but they'll always be lacking a certain dimension.

Peter is talking to Selma outside. His arms are crossed and his lips are moving without pause. Selma's eyes are gazing up at the cloudless sky. The boys are nowhere to be seen; Rahel can only hear their voices.

Then she gets up and goes outside.

"Theo! Max!" she calls. "Come on, let's go to the lake."

The boys come running and Peter gives her a look of gratitude.

□

All afternoon Selma seems to be avoiding them. She's also cool towards the children. She goes to the bathroom and spends ages there, then back to the boulder to reconnect with the outside world, as she says. She slips out while the children are eating blancmange with raspberries and doesn't come back for a full hour. Without explanation.

"Leave her," Peter says. "She's digesting it all." Besides, he adds, he gets the impression that for the first time in her life Selma's developing some ambition. So they can't dismiss it out of hand.

Selma's lack of ambition was a real problem while she was at school. If she got a D in a test she wasn't at all disappointed, announcing with her disarming smile that you had to know half the content to get a D, and half was quite a lot. Selma got angry when Rahel was concerned and asked why she should be content with the minimum rather than striving for the best. When Selma got older she accused Rahel of only loving her when she did well. There were arduous discussions, long evenings at the kitchen table with tears and reproach, followed by sleepless nights. The outcome was worthless. Whereas they had to keep reining in Simon's ambition, Selma seemed to lack any at all.

It was also around the time that Selma began to dress really provocatively. Her get-up made virtually everyone turn their head. Selma referred to those whose eyes lingered on her for more than a second as fucking perverts, and when Peter encouraged her to dress at least halfway normally for school, and Rahel dared ask if Selma thought it would be a good thing if her male teachers turned up to class with their penises hanging out, her response was a snort of indignation and a scornful laugh.

They sat it out by treating it like an illness – with patience and a lump in the throat. Every day they hoped their daughter would make it home unscathed and that this phase would pass. And it did. Like so many other phases.

Simon, who didn't cause half as much fuss, didn't get half as much attention either. He sailed through puberty, getting drunk a few times and occasionally not coming home at the agreed time. That was it. Sport was at the centre of his life. School didn't cause him any problems. To Peter's regret he spurned literature, but would read every history book their home library had to offer.

Rahel isn't surprised that her memory is dominated by Selma. And by Selma's friends, who came in and out of their apartment as gaggles of girls. They would besiege the kitchen, hold cooking and baking orgies, listen to loud music and put the rest of the family to flight. They clustered in the bathroom to dye their hair, ruining towels, polluting the room with the stench of bleaching products, and when they bumped into her in the corridor they'd whisper *Hello, Frau Wunderlich* in saccharine voices. For hours they would occupy the balcony, at some point shooting off in a pack, but not before making a big hoo-ha about their goodbyes. Often – and these were the worst days of all – they would have a sleepover in Selma's room and plunder the fridge in the night.

If Simon had friends over, it was only ever one and they would go to his room. He'd close the door and they'd stay there.

❑

Late in the afternoon, before the adults' supper, Theo and Max are happily munching fusilli with tomato sauce. Rahel watches them, exhausted.

At least they're sitting down. At the table.

Max picks up a spiral and tries to stretch it. When it breaks he chucks it on the floor.

"No!" Rahel says sternly.

"Leave my brother alone!" Theo says, sounding angry.

Meanwhile Max is dropping more bits of pasta on the floor. Theo smacks his fingers hard and bellows, "No!"

This playing to the gallery speaks volumes, but Rahel keeps tight-lipped.

Just this last evening. And a morning. Then peace will return.

Week Two

Monday

Selma's by the radio holding a cup of coffee. She's got it on so loud that the newsreader is drowning out the children.

Rahel makes a beeline for the device and turns it down. She doesn't want to listen.

"Anything new happened in the world?" she asks, trying to sound as relaxed as possible.

"Hardly any women in management positions, that's what," Selma announces angrily. "Men are clinging to power. It's unbelievable. Germany comes off really badly. Worse than Poland!"

"Well . . ." Rahel says encouragingly.

Selma raises her eyebrows in suspicion.

"What's stopping a young woman like you from studying business and landing a top job?" Rahel asks, and even as she utters these words she senses it would have been better to keep quiet.

"Excuse me!" Selma says sourly, pointing at Theo and Max who are sitting beneath the table, eating their porridge.

"Aha," Rahel says. She squats and says sweetly, "Right, you little career wreckers. How about you sit up with me?"

"You can't help yourself, can you?" Now Selma sounds tired. "You always have to run me down."

Sighing, Rahel stands up and takes a step towards her

daughter. "I just want to show you that it's more complicated than it may seem. It's not just a male thirst for power at play here, but also the life decisions that women make."

"Well, say that then, rather than attacking me. You wouldn't talk to Simon like that."

Rahel can feel the shame warming her cheeks. Selma's right. On the other hand, Simon doesn't talk such nonsense. Her daughter's naivety is crying out to be rectified. This division of humanity into offenders and victims! This childish view of the world!

"I'm sorry," she says to Selma nonetheless, to avoid ruining the last few hours they have together.

Theo and Max leave their bowls under the table and run outside. They come back in again almost immediately and grab hold of Rahel and Selma, looking serious and shocked, their eyes like saucers. Outside in the yard they point to what's made them so agitated. Lying on the lid of an old plastic bin are frozen day-old chicks and mice, which the stork will have later. The boys have removed the mesh dome that Peter had put over the pile of dead animals and now it's attracting the cats and insects.

"All dead," Theo declares with a shrug.

Later they watch impassively as the stork eats. Selma takes a few pictures with her phone and says, out of the blue, "We could stay a few more days, you know."

Peter slowly raises his head. Then he answers with a calm but firm "No".

Nothing more. Just this clear, all-embracing *No*.

□

With their departure imminent, Peter paces nervously around the yard. He keeps looking around for Selma who *just wanted to pop down to the lake again.* The boys are in the car, pressing their noses against the windows. They're not going to put up with this for much longer. Eventually Selma wanders back, deliberately slowly, looking pained and reproachful.

Rahel strokes her arm. "Come on, there's no point putting it off. You and Vincent have got to talk and get some help."

"Time to go!" Peter says, holding open the door for her. Then they drive out of the yard, Rahel following them as far as the boulder, waving all the while.

This is exactly what Viktor and Ruth used to do. Viktor would usually be a few metres behind Ruth, and when Ruth had stopped waving and turned to go back to the house, he'd stay there, eyes fixed and arm raised. Rahel would always hang over the back seat of the Trabi, shouting "Byeeee!" over and over again to the ever-diminishing figure. Every year Tamara would say "Don't shout so loudly! You're annoying!", before burrowing deep in her seat, while Edith tried to keep a steady hand on the wheel, her eyes blurred with tears.

Rahel's stomach cramps with anxiety. But is it the memories or the here and now that's tying her insides in knots? She can't tell.

She walks back to the house, deep in thought. There's no denying it, Selma's departure is a relief. But the relief is cancelled out by her bad conscience, and what remains is the sense of having failed.

Slowly Rahel goes up the stairs. Everything here suddenly looks shabby – the dirty walls, the scuffed wooden steps, the worn handrail. Cracked tiles, cupboards that don't shut, windows that are never cleaned.

She tortures herself with a few pages of the novel the bookseller back home raved about, but she's not taken by the story.

Rahel paces the room, peers out of the window, sees the

stork and the one-eared cat, and imagines the animals are staring back at her with hostility.

It feels as though Peter is gone for an age and she is dragged into a profound melancholy. Outside the sun is searing. As if in a stop-motion film it scorches everything that is green and blooming. Rahel ought to have watered early this morning.

Pulling herself together, she wanders to the mailbox that's outside the property, fixed to a thick wooden stake. It's big enough to take packages and has a lid that's sealed with a felted roof to prevent rain or snow getting in. Viktor and Ruth reduced the risk of unwanted human contact to a minimum – a way of living that's very much to Peter's taste too. The box is empty. Rahel strolls around the buildings, watches the chickens in their fenced-off garden, picks a few dried leaves from bushes and shrubs and imagines how it would be to live here for ever. The summers would be wonderful, but from October till April there would be nothing but endless work, bleak winter days, freezing rooms, stinking animals and always the same clothes. Most of her wardrobe would be useless here. Unsuitable for the house and garden. Too extravagant for the village.

If she were in Ruth's shoes she wouldn't go to the same effort, making herself up every day with lipstick and mascara, and standing up straight, shoulders back. No, Rahel would probably let herself go.

She looks for a bench in the shade and sits down. Closing her eyes she dozes for a while until she hears the car, its door closing and Peter approaching with cautious steps.

"I came back via the shops. And brought us something hot to eat. Vietnamese, I think."

Rahel smiles wearily and follows him into the kitchen

where a pungent aroma soon billows from the opened foil cartons.

"Do you want to know what Selma told me?"

"I'd rather not."

"About the electroacoustic installer," Peter says, ignoring her wishes. "He's got four children of his own."

"With how many women?"

"Two."

Rahel pushes her food to one side.

"You could have told me later. Now I've lost my appetite."

Peter takes his chopsticks from their paper wrapper and holds them awkwardly between his fingers.

"She says he inspires her."

"And what did you say?"

"That it's fine for her to be inspired, but she doesn't have to let it destroy her family."

Rahel stares at him.

"So you advised her to have an affair?"

"Not in so many words. But yes, I tried to make her understand that these things can happen. That feelings ebb and flow, and she shouldn't make any rash decisions."

"I see," says Rahel, dumbfounded. If only he'd been so understanding of her that time.

Fifteen years ago she cheated on him while at a systemic therapy training course. With Alex, a psychologist, coach and former competitive swimmer. A man who asked her straight out if she fancied going to bed with him. She'd caught his eye and immediately he'd wanted to sleep with her. If she felt the same she should give him a sign – something, a message, a glance. The conference hotel was on the edge of the Taunus mountain range, and she'd intended to go walking in her spare time. Three days with barely any sleep while Peter held the fort with the children at home. He sent her messages that she answered curtly and mechanically: *I'm fine too. I'm thinking of you and missing you all. Kisses to you and the children.* The words simply came trotting out while her body glowed. She hadn't been aware just how dark her desire was.

And then, back in Dresden, her unnecessary confession, Peter's horror and his agonising silence that went on for months.

Food keeps falling from his chopsticks. Covering her container with its aluminium lid, Rahel puts it in the fridge.

"I'll eat later," she says, leaving the room.

◻

She avoids him till the evening. The shimmering heat paralyses all activity. No birds are singing, the cats have crawled away to hidey-holes, the stork stands still in a shady spot in the yard. Peter has withdrawn to his dark room. He's perfectly happy with the company of writers. The easiest way to grab his attention is via the books he reads. When she engages with subjects he's reading about, wonderful conversations ensue, even after all their years of marriage. But right now she has no energy or interest even for that.

She strolls over to the chicken garden and watches the hens take dust baths. They roll around in the shade of two apple trees, clucking and ruffling their feathers. A buzzard is circling high above. Beyond the chicken garden is the path to the paddock. It's lined with ancient cherry and plum trees, some already dead. Amongst them are two mirabelles, wasps buzzing around their ripe fruit. Ruth once told her that these were *early mirabelle Bergthold* – a name that has the ring of old nobility.

Baila is standing beneath a tree, right beside the water

trough. She flicks the flies away with her tail and waggles her ears. They're all doing what they have to – every chicken and every horse, and Peter obviously. Only Rahel doesn't know what to do. She can't abide herself on this torpefying hot day. She wishes someone would come and lift the burden of her own existence from her shoulders, even for a few hours.

Tuesday

"It's astonishing," Peter says when Rahel comes into the kitchen at eight o'clock, "how prescient Pasolini was."

"Good morning," she replies, then fills the kettle and shakes ground coffee into the cafetière.

"Fifty-five years ago," he continues unperturbed, "he wrote about how culture was destroyed by the consumer society."

For a few seconds his lecture is drowned out by the kettle and he stops. When Rahel sits opposite him, a slice of toast on her plate, he resumes. She knows the topic; they've talked about it many times. It's one of the things they both believe in implicitly: universalism and uniformity on every level are noble goals with fatal consequences. A diverse world rich in culture is increasingly being homogenised; the unusual and distinct is being destroyed. All that remains is consumption.

She can't count the number of evenings she and Peter have discussed this, but like everything Rahel has regarded as doomed, one day her interest died. She doesn't revolt against the inevitable; she saves her energy for more useful battles.

But still she listens to him as she drinks her coffee. His eyes are gleaming. Peter has always maintained this insatiable thirst for knowledge.

"Pasolini calls consumption the new fascism," Peter says, leafing through the slim volume, putting his finger on the relevant page and reading out loud. He invests everything in his passion for thinking, and Rahel has to admit that she has learned a lot from him in this respect.

In the early days of their relationship they often read the same books and talked about them afterwards. They'd spend evenings tackling particular topics, either just the two of them or with friends. Peter would always ask her to remain detached and then to look at the issue from different perspectives. It was a training of the mind that she happily participated in and finds useful to this day.

Even now he tries to teach his students this form of free thinking and reflection on one's own opinions – with decreasing success and growing frustration. The virus and the restrictions it imposed came at an opportune moment for Peter. In the summer semester his presence in the university building was no longer required. He did what was necessary by video conference and lost interest in the rest.

"You'd have been better off teaching philosophy, not literature," she remarks with a smile. "I think you're always asking too much of your students."

He looks up, surprised, then takes off his glasses and frowns. "Anyone who embarks on a humanities degree ought to be interested in the process of thinking itself, don't you agree?"

"Of course!" she says. "But you have an idealised picture of erudite students from a long-gone era, when university study was the exception rather than the rule."

"You're right," he says with a smile. Putting his glasses on he says, to her surprise, "Do I get a coffee too?"

Rahel fetches a cup from the cupboard. On the side it says *Hmm . . .* She pours him coffee and is delighted when he smiles.

She experiences a faint hint of the old days, and she remembers what she always says to estranged couples to begin with: *Do you remember when you were in love? What was it about your husband/wife that you loved?*

Rahel can answer this question effortlessly: Peter's intelligence, his attractiveness, his reliability and his humour.

He's lost none of these and that's why she doesn't want to lose him.

She knows what it's like out there. The highly competitive market for partners is quite demanding for those on the hunt. The "goods" are used and damaged. They have their quirks and flaws, illnesses and anxieties, and usually they're lacking in flexibility. Those who start from the beginning again at fifty find people who've grown with others, been formed by others – bent into shape, trimmed and no longer prepared to bend or be bent again. Both she and Peter would want someone to take them as they are. For decades they've balanced each other out. They've come far together.

If Rahel is asked how long she's been married, she reveals the figure with a touch of pride. Barely any of the couples they've met during their marriage have made it to their silver anniversary, and even Selma and Simon have at some point acknowledged the value of their stable relationship. Sadly this awareness doesn't extend to imitation, as Selma is currently proving. And as for Simon, his girlfriends can stay on the scene so long as they don't disturb his training schedule. If they want more, they have to go.

Peter clicks his fingers. "What are you thinking about?"

"Our children," Rahel says with a deep sigh.

"You look like you're in pain," he says with a smirk.

"Well . . . there's Selma with her histrionics and Simon whose sheer ambition and discipline makes him forget to live."

Peter pulls a face that's meant to tell her: You're exaggerating.

"What's got you onto this?"

She brushes him off. "I can't explain."

Pushing his cup to one side he reaches across the table for her hand.

"Don't turn our children into patients. Simon's getting on fine, and Selma—"

"We should never have given Selma to your mother when she was a baby," Rahel interrupts, pulling her hand back abruptly. "Her behaviour shows clear symptoms of infantile attachment disorder."

"Maybe. But tell me, who doesn't have attachment disorder. You've definitely got it, and as for me . . ." He smiles bitterly. "I really wish my mother had been as loving to me as she was to Selma."

He leans forwards and tries to catch her gaze.

"Selma doesn't need you to analyse her, Rahel. She needs you to be her mother."

As if she didn't know that. But there's a hurdle between knowledge and action, and she doesn't always have the strength to overcome it.

□

"We're not the only ones who come here to swim," Peter says, pointing with his foot at a used face mask in the sand. Then he wades naked into the water. For the first time she notices the small rolls of fat on his lower back. When did she last see him naked, actually? But before she can take a closer look he dives under the surface.

Rahel sits on her towel and notices the cigarette butts to her left. They've been stuck in the sand in a heart shape. In the best of all worlds – an intellectual game she often plays with Peter – nobody would leave their rubbish lying around like that. She gathers the butts into a tissue and thinks of the cigarette in the studio. This evening she'll smoke it over a glass of wine, without making a secret of it. Peter can think what he likes.

She sees him far out in the lake, bobbing up and down at regular intervals. He's going to be fifty-five on Sunday. She still doesn't have a present for him.

Rahel removes her dress and underwear and looks around. She can't see anybody. Slowly she makes her way into the lake. The water is so clear that she can see the bottom. Schools of tiny fish swim past her. She wants to swim towards Peter, at least some of the way. In the best of all worlds he'd put his hands on her body and kiss her until they both sank.

Peter doesn't seem to have noticed her; he's swimming on his back, churning up the water with his arms and legs. She calls out but he can't hear. It's only when she's level with him that she catches his eye.

"You've come a long way out today," he calls. For a few seconds he treads water, delighted by how clean the lake is and how beautiful the view of the woods all around, then he swims breaststroke the rest of the way back. She watches him get out of the water and dry himself. He stretches and turns his face to the sun for a few seconds.

The best of all worlds is a game for fantasists.

□

For lunch he serves her a colourful salad with crumbled feta. The salad bowl is pure anarchy: peppers diced into tiny pieces alongside finger-thick slices of cucumber.

"Was that your attempt to do something crazy?" she says a touch too snappily.

He grins and fills her plate.

"Do you want to spend all three weeks on the farm?"

He shrugs. "I don't see any reason to move from here."

"We could go on a trip."

"Where to?" He chews and shakes his head. "It's lovely here."

They have twelve more days ahead of them. To give the afternoon a bit of structure, Rahel plans to ring Ruth, take a walk, find out what's going on with Selma and then discuss it with Peter.

◻

"Rahel," Ruth says in a weary voice.

"Yes, it's me," Rahel says unnecessarily. She asks after Viktor and listens to Ruth's sober account of the drama that's being played out in marvellous weather in Ahrenshoop.

Viktor is struggling to deal with what lies ahead. He's always said that he didn't think a life like that worth living, and now he wants her to help him end it. Yes, Rahel heard correctly. End it. But of course she can't do that. And nor does she want to. But in a moment of weakness many years ago she gave him her word, and now he's constantly reminding her of it.

Ruth's voice is quavering and Rahel realises that her own questions about Viktor will have to wait. Once again she has to be patient.

With Ruth she still behaves like a child. She has nothing to counter this woman's authority. As a psychologist she ought to be able to come up with an appropriate response to Viktor's problem, but aside from a few *I sees*, *reallys*, and *oh dears*, Rahel hardly manages to utter a word.

All the same she makes Ruth promise to keep her posted.

"It'll be fine," Ruth says at the end, and her *Bye-bye, my love!* sounds as it always does.

○

Rahel stands beside the telephone for a while longer.

According to her schedule it's time for her walk.

"Come on then!" she says aloud to herself. "Pull yourself together." Suddenly she feels as if Ruth's severe gaze has travelled all the way here. Rahel promptly leaves the house and sets off.

She stops by the paddock. Baila seems to know not to expect anything from Rahel. She doesn't dignify her with a look.

"Tell Peter to stop being such a snowflake!" Rahel says to the grazing mare, and continues her walk. Then she turns around once more. "And don't let him think I'm going to wait around for him for ever!"

Baila raises her head slightly, but then freezes in this new position, as if dozing.

With long strides Rahel hurries into the woods, driven by a helpless anger. She wants to scream, and before she can change her mind she does so, several times in succession, yelling at the top of her voice.

○

"You're back!" Peter calls out, sounding relieved.

He's standing by the stable door, Baila's halter and a length of rope over his shoulder.

"I was worried. I heard screaming in the woods."

"Some people were arguing," she mutters.

"Sounded dreadful."

"Yes, well," she says with a shrug, then adds as she walks off, "I'm going to call Selma."

"Good idea," he says. "I'm going to take the horse out."

In the kitchen Rahel opens the door to the pantry and

her gaze falls on the homemade jams. She picks up a small jar of quince jelly, opens it and gives it a sniff. Then she spreads a slice of bread with butter and heaps onto it spoonfuls of jelly, demolishing the entire jar. Her teeth ache from the overpowering sweetness. Not a single tooth in her mouth is sound, and she's already lost three. She's got Edith to thank for that; they were always allowed sugary peppermint tea with lemon, as much sweetened fried bread as they wanted and sometimes half a grapefruit with sugar sprinkled on top. The acid dissolved the enamel and the sugar ate into their young, beautiful teeth, ruining them one after another.

□

Selma doesn't answer. Rahel's tried three times now. She texts her daughter, asking her to call back. The longer the silence, the angrier she becomes.

Unlike Edith, Rahel made sure that her daughter paid regular visits to the dentist, that her enamel was strengthened with Elmex gel and that the cracks in her molars were filled. The least she can expect after so much care is a call back.

She lies on her bed, closes her eyes and takes deep breaths to banish the anger.

There is no fury mingled with the worry when she's waiting for Simon's calls. Her feelings for him are different. Peter knows it, Selma senses it, only Simon is clueless.

Does she love him more? She asks the question out loud and honestly, as if her voice were a second person in the room. The truth is, she loves him differently. He never triggers anything in her she'd have to feel ashamed about. Her love for this child flows purely and without pause.

Finally the phone rings.

"Hello," Vincent says. "Selma asked me to call you. She's gone for a bit of a lie-down."

"Is everything alright?"

"Depends how you look at it."

Rahel can hear the squeal of a tram in the background. Vincent pre-empts her question.

"I'm on the way to the playground with the children."

"Have you . . . spoken to each other?" she asks circumspectly.

"All morning." He lowers his voice. "The boys are listening and I don't want—"

"Sure! I can call back later."

"No, wait! I told her that what she's feeling now might not last, and that she can't just take the boys to Leipzig with her. They're my children too, Rahel."

"Of course!" she says.

"I think we'll work it out. I . . ."

Then he tells her how he proposes to convince Selma. Rahel finds his emotional maturity remarkable.

Life with her daughter is like permanently swimming upstream. At some point Rahel stopped kicking against it. But Vincent is young and strong; maybe he won't go under in her wild waters.

□

Afterwards, sitting on a bench in the garden, she tries in vain to lose herself in Viktor's pilgrim book. It bores her; she's only reading it because she thinks she'll find out something about him.

One of the many cats has settled on the bench beside her.

Its low purring strengthens her desire to close her eyes and not think of anything.

Then she sees Peter with a beaming smile.

"Baila comes when I call her now," he says excitedly. "And she walks beside me without the halter."

"Oh . . . how lovely," she says, suppressing a yawn.

He walks off with a spring in his step, leaving her feeling completely superfluous. Rahel opens the book again.

Even Edith had a copy of the Bible on her shelves, and Rahel used to read it like a book of fairy tales – with interest, but sure in the knowledge that it was all made up. Her one and only religious experience was a few years ago on a trip to the US, when they attended a Free Church service. Even before she was inside the hall she could hear the people filing in, almost all them black, saying *God is good!* to which the answer was always *All the time!* During the sermon the congregation would stand after every phrase they liked and call out *Amen!* or *Hallelujah!* and raise their hands and dance. Then came the singing. The tears streamed down Rahel's face. Peter made fun of her, describing the whole thing as the perfect show, a pretty jamboree. But there had been a degree of genuineness about it, and this gave Rahel the sense that something inside her was lacking, and it dogged her for the rest of the trip.

She puts the pilgrim's tales definitively aside and feels the callouses on her hands. The gardening has left its mark. Her hands could do with a a little care. She can see more age marks too. At her last dermatological check-up the doctor asked if she had once been a sun-worshipper. Her skin was showing the usual damage caused by excessive sunbathing. She shrugged, hoping he'd put away his magnifying glass and let her go. Having her blemishes examined was an unpleasant experience and she felt sorry for the man. It must be horrible, she thought, to have to check people's skin day in day out for pathological changes.

□

She avoids Peter until suppertime.

"Did you speak to Selma?" he says when she joins him at the kitchen table.

She shakes her head. "No, but I did talk to Vincent. He's optimistic, as ever."

Peter smiles. "He's a great chap."

"Maybe . . ." she says, but points out that Selma isn't behaving like this for no reason.

"I just wonder how weighty her reasons are," he says.

Rahel doesn't respond. From her perspective the reasons are neither pressing nor significant, but so what? Over the past few years she's seen more and more young people at her practice who can't cope with their lives. And these are educated people with money and loving parents. For reasons that are hard to understand they end their relationships, throw in their careers, break off their studies just before the end, and feel unhappy. As if a good life were a heavy burden. Because anyone who is handed it all on a plate and yet makes nothing of it can't expect to be met with sympathy.

"The burden of a good life," she says, hoping that Peter will understand her without the need for further explanation.

And he does.

"These days young people's lives are difficult in different ways," he says.

Their eyes meet and stay fixed on each other. For a moment Rahel believes that everything will take a turn for the better.

Wednesday

Almost.

Peter almost stayed with her. Yesterday evening, in her room, her bed.

Like in the old days when they were young, they sat on the floor, Peter with one leg stretched out and the other tucked in, Rahel cross-legged. They talked about the seven virtues – prudence, justice, fortitude, temperance, faith, hope and love – and questioned whether temperance applied to knowledge too. After the second glass of wine they'd come to the conclusion that although education was essential for an understanding of the world, there was definitely a point where prudence tipped over into stupidity. Someone who was no longer able to react spontaneously, who first had to painstakingly put everything they experienced in a theoretical context, had reached that tipping point.

"They ignore instinct and anxiety that serves a purpose. Knowledge becomes their undoing and ultimately they flounder," Rahel stated, and Peter concluded that everything could become destructive, absolutely everything. Then she took the glass from his hand and pulled him up onto the bed.

For a while he lay there on his back, holding her in his arms. His eyes were open, staring at the ceiling, while she waited for him to utter a tender word. She fancied she could already sense the word, see it forming and making its way to her. Rahel adjusted her breathing to his to remove the last residue of resistance that could get in the word's way. Very gently he pulled his arm out from underneath her, kissed her and left the bedroom.

□

At around two o'clock she woke up, her heart racing, and so sweaty that she had to change. In her dream she'd seen Simon lying dead in a field, but the dream wasn't responsible for the state she was in. These night-time visitations, often accompanied by a sudden terror, had been plaguing her for at least a year, always at the same time, between two and three in the morning, sometimes with nausea, sometimes without, occasionally with an inexplicable itching all over her body, and always with a racing heart and profuse sweating. The smell of the sweat was bad, too – sour and pungent. She never used to smell like that. These nasty side effects of getting older would at least make it easier one day to let go of this life.

And with this thought in her head she had fallen asleep again.

□

Prudence, justice, fortitude, temperance, faith, hope and love.

She'd written all seven virtues in a column on a piece of paper and circled fortitude.

Today she's going to be brave. She'll deal bravely with Peter's coldness, which isn't a real coldness but a mixture of oddity, lack of confidence and the loss of an affinity with others. When he began to turn his back on society she didn't follow suit. She didn't do anything to help him. And when the disconcertment grew in her too, Peter was already gone – into an inner refuge whose door wasn't easy to open. A simpler man wouldn't have had such sensibilities, but nor would a simpler man have loved her in the way he does.

Beneath her window she hears fierce hissing. Leaning out, she sees a large tabby tomcat scurry away with a bird in its jaws. It irks Rahel that they hunt. Every morning and evening Peter fills their bowls with the best cat food, and yet every few days a bird is killed. She closes the window, grabs a towel, slips on her pumps and heads for the lake.

His towel, shirt and trousers are hanging from a branch that reaches out over the water. His shoes are neatly placed below it. Her gaze sweeps the lake; the water lies tranquil and sleek before her. Peter is probably doing the big loop around the bay to the left.

Half of the holiday is over.

She pokes her toes into the sand. At a stroke all her worries now seem ridiculous. Of course Peter and she will come to an understanding. Of course Selma will do the right thing and of course nothing will happen to Simon. *Have faith, Rahel*, she tells herself silently. *You have to have faith*. Then she lets her gaze wander again across the still surface of the water.

He's a good swimmer. But even endurance swimmers get cramps or heart attacks. She hangs her dress over the branch with his things, puts her shoes beside his, enters the water and starts swimming.

Beyond a sizeable oasis of waterlilies, which she's never swum to before, lies a tiny bay. There, in the shallow water, he's sitting with his head back and eyes closed. Rahel stops swimming. He doesn't seem to have heard her. Behind him is an uninterrupted mass of reeds.

Rahel turns carefully. With each movement she makes an effort to keep her arms under water, to avoid splashing.

This moment is his alone.

On her way to the garden centre her mobile pings several times. She waits till she gets to the car park.

Simon has sent some pictures. Her son in full climbing gear on some rock face, dramatic clouds in the sky. Simon with just a hand clutching a mountain ledge, the rest of his body dangling over the abyss. In the next picture he's using both hands and a foot is perched on a tiny ledge. The last one shows a view of the valley from the top. The rock face looks smooth and vertical. It's a mystery to her how he got up there.

Simon can't accept being normal either. He sets his goals ever higher. It's not just the endorphin rush he gets from the immense freedom of climbing – like Selma he can't stand mediocrity.

Rahel stares across the car park. What is wrong with her children? Or does her job prevent her from having a dispassionate view.

She puts on a face mask, takes a trolley and wanders up and down the aisles. A sales assistant gives her advice on drought-resistant plants and Rahel plumps for the large-flowered coreopsis and a pink-flowering sedum.

Rahel thinks about the lush plants on her balcony at home and hopes that her neighbour Frau Knopp hasn't forgotten to water them.

Frau Knopp never goes on holiday. She reliably takes in their packages, asks after the children and is always bang up to date on Dresden city politics. In winter she sometimes stands and smokes by the bike racks behind the building, wrapped up in an old parka and a bobble hat she knitted herself. In summer she virtually lives on the balcony of her raised ground-floor apartment. She must be well over eighty, but she dresses in bold colours and striking patterns.

When Selma was a little girl she once said to her, "I don't want to get as old as you." In response to Frau Knopp's question as to how she was going to avoid it, she said, "Die." Frau Knopp burst out laughing, and Selma just laughed with her.

In return for looking after Rahel's plants, Frau Knopp was genuinely modest, asking for "a bottle or two of red wine, but no Dornfelder and nothing under five euros."

□

The word "wine" makes Rahel think of food. At the checkout she asks the cashier where the nearest butcher is, then quickly grabs a spray bottle she spots in a special offers basket beside the till and puts it on the conveyer belt. Back outside, she puts the plants in the footwell by the passenger seat and follows the directions she's been given to Thiel's, the butcher.

She buys fillets of lamb, then picks up garlic, rosemary, clarified butter and corn salad from the grocery, a baguette from the bakery and heads back feeling relaxed. It's easy to please Peter with good food. In spring, when the virus meant there were no in-person classes at the university, but Rahel was swamped with work at her practice, he started cooking. Since then he appreciates the effort even more. He sticks pedantically to the recipes in the cookbooks and now makes some impressive dishes, but without detailed instructions he's lost.

Rahel never uses cookbooks. She opens the fridge, takes out everything that needs using up and improvises.

□

Back in Dorotheenfelde she unpacks the bags and searches in vain for Peter. She wrote him a note before heading into town; he hasn't left anything for her.

In his room she sits at the desk, unashamedly leafing through his notebook. He's been copying out quotations from books for as long as she can remember. Usually they're things he likes, but he also jots down viewpoints he doesn't agree with at all, adding his own thoughts. In his narrow, perfectly legible handwriting that slants slightly to the right, it says: *The woodland wanderer is the person who has a primal relationship with freedom* (. . .)

Nobody else she knows has this connection with literature. Peter doesn't just read books, he works with them, relates what he's read to himself, his views, his behaviour and changes them if necessary. For him, literature is like a living counterpart. Sometimes even more alive than what plays out before his eyes. And unlike people, he finds it indispensable.

Closing his notebook with a sigh, she leaves his room, goes downstairs and steps outside into the yard.

Peter comes around the corner.

"You're back already!" he calls out. "I was so absorbed by this pilgrim book," he says when he's standing beside her.

"Pilgrim book?"

He nods. "It was on the bench over there in the garden. I've always wanted to read it. Salinger refers to it in *Franny and Zooey* . . . It's a shame we can't ask Viktor what the book means to him."

"Yes, shame," she replies softly. "There are all sorts of things I'd like to ask him."

When he doesn't respond to her remark, she strides past him towards the studio and calls back, "Come on, there's something I've got to show you."

□

"Don't jump to any rash conclusions," Peter warns her after

he's seen all those pictures of Edith and Rahel. "He drew the both of you – so what? You often came here."

"But he hardly spent any time with Tamara, he was almost only ever with me."

Peter cocks his head. "Look, I didn't know Tamara as a child, but she's not an easy person, your sister. Besides, you know yourself that attractive people often get more love, and you were an exceptionally pretty little girl."

He looks at a drawing of Edith.

"Do you believe your mother could have done that? Taken a secret like that to the grave? Betray her best friend by having an affair with her husband and never allow a child to know her father?"

Without hesitation Rahel says, "Yes."

The large tabby crosses the yard, a mouse twitching in its mouth.

The sun blazes mercilessly at its zenith. The leaves of the large elder that covers the window of Peter's room are drooping, and even the sparrows that populate it in great numbers seem to have been put into a state of semi-consciousness by the heat. Rahel glances at the plants she bought today and watered in the shade.

"I understand that you need to know," Peter says, putting his arms around her from behind. He pulls her towards him and holds her tight for a long moment; and the longer he holds her, the less urgent becomes her need to know.

□

Later, when the two of them have retired to their rooms for an afternoon rest, it's back, hammering away at the inside of her skull. She goes to the window and stares for a while at the woods, which are numbed by the heat.

What if it never rains again? she suddenly thinks. What if the lake that now shimmers between the trees dries up? The edge of the shore has receded. When she was a child the water extended further. What if soon the lake no longer exists?

She would love to be spared these thoughts. This everything's-always-getting-worse fear. But it can't be argued away – the forests are dying, the ice is melting and people aren't getting any smarter. And because there are so many people, more than ever, and increasing in number all the time, the damage they're causing is becoming incalculable.

Already in spring it occurred to them that the pandemic might be nothing but a long overdue corrective.

"Imagine," Peter said, "that the excessive increase in the global population makes nature decimate it. Let's say by half. Through a virus, for example."

The idea made sense. Of course it mustn't affect her and her family, and in the end the rampant virus didn't have anything like the impact Peter had envisioned, but the idea of a corrective remained compelling. If it were true, their entire existence and everything they did would be even more insignificant and superfluous than they already assumed. Peter often soars to these lofty heights, gazing down at everything from above, then returns to the lowlands of everyday life with an indulgent smile.

She runs her hand a few times over her black linen dress, which she's now wearing for the tenth day in a row. Touching the robust material, she feels a strangely grim pleasure in not having to attach any importance to outward appearance.

❑

Later she goes for another swim. The little bay where Peter had been sitting is now in sunshine. Rahel swims until she can feel the sandy ground with her hands. She turns around, sits in the tepid shallow water, supports herself on her arms and holds her face to the sun. Endless iridescent dragonflies buzz around her.

This moment belongs to her. And despite all the gloomy thoughts it is complete and perfect.

□

In the evening, after Peter has fed the animals, Rahel has planted the coreopsis and sedum and watered the other plants, she fries the fillets of lamb in plenty of clarified butter with garlic and rosemary. Peter makes the salad, slices the baguette and opens a bottle of wine. Despite the wasps they eat outside. The trick with the spray bottle works; as soon as a wasp approaches, Rahel covers it in a fine mist. Peter grins, then reaches for the bottle himself. He sprays water boisterously in all directions. Even the stork gets a squirt, as do the cats, who are begging for food.

"You've already had yours!" Peter says like a strict father, shooing them away.

They finish the bottle of red wine and a large carafe of water, and when Peter asks if he should open another bottle Rahel nods.

At around midnight there are three empty wine bottles on the table. Rahel staggers upstairs while Peter tidies up. Without cleaning her teeth or putting in her night guard she lies on the bed and falls asleep in an instant.

Thursday

What angers her most about the state she's in is how predictable it is. The throbbing pain in her head, the incredible thirst, the terrible taste in her dry mouth and the diarrhoea – at the age of almost fifty, she still doesn't have enough common sense to prevent it all.

Of course she was wide awake after about two hours of comatose sleep – sweating, and with her heart beating wildly. The night was as ghastly as the evening was lovely. Fortunately she has her own bathroom where she can fully indulge her wretched state.

❏

In the kitchen she makes some strong coffee and takes it upstairs with a large bottle of mineral water. One thing is for certain: she's not going to become an alcoholic. A single hangover is enough to keep her away from large quantities of booze for a long time. She can't remember what they talked about at the end; all she knows is that they laughed a lot and shooting stars went racing across the sky.

There's a knock at the door and Peter pokes his head round.

"How are you feeling?" he says.

The look on his face tells her that his night was just as bad. Rahel rocks her head and grimaces.

"I see," he mumbles, adding, "Me too."

He closes the door, then opens it again immediately and says, "Nice evening, though!"

When he's gone, a scrap of the conversation they had comes back to her. She asked him which period in history he'd like to travel to.

"Antiquity!" he said at once. "But before the itinerant preacher got up to mischief."

When she understood what he was getting at, they both exploded with laughter and, tears streaming down her face, Rahel prophesised that there would now be a lightning strike, a raincloud emptying on top of them, or birds crapping on their heads.

□

While Peter swims a loop in the lake to sober up, Rahel tries to avoid all unnecessary movement. Her eyes closed, she remains in a half-sitting, half-lying position, and to cap it all her teeth are aching.

Around lunchtime she feels well enough to leave the room. Muggy and overcast, the day seems to match her mood. No bright light, no sharp shadows, just a soft warmth without the risk of sunburn.

For a while she sits on the bench right beside the front door, taking sips of Peter's favourite summer drink – green tea that's been chilled in the fridge for at least an hour. It's healthy and full of minerals. He brought the special glass pot with in-built filter from home.

Rahel thinks rather apprehensively of their return to Dresden and the autumn and winter ahead, when the virus might surge again, when new measures will be announced that rescind the advantages of city life, and her appointment schedule will be bursting once more.

Back in spring she'd already observed an increase in depression. She gave some of these patients reading recommendations, from Viktor E. Frankl's *Man's Search for Meaning* to Wolfgang Herrndorf's *Work and Structure*. But that was only for those who merely needed a nudge in the right direction.

She thinks of the evening when they watched *Melancholia*.

"I know that feeling," Peter had said.

Clients like Peter are hopeless cases. They know the reason for their problem – their intelligence has enabled them to self-analyse – and they've ruled out being cured. For the conditions they need cannot be manufactured. In the era into which they're born they can't find what they're looking for: meaningfulness and dignity instead of personal fulfilment, and a society in which the aim isn't to live as long as possible, but to shape one's life as constructively as possible.

When concern about the virus escalated, they talked about this often. Both are of the firm belief that a life lived in permanent fear is worthless.

And yet Rahel was less certain when it came to dealing with the virus. Panic and calm alternated week by week, depending on how often she listened to the news. The infection and death rates definitely had an effect, and it wasn't until she complied with Peter's irritated request to spare herself the daily dose of horror and use her reason that she felt better.

A few years ago she and Peter made living wills. Neither of them wanted any life-support, artificial nutrition, resuscitation or artificial respiration. The only thing they consented to was pain relief. They told the children where they kept the documents and Peter claimed that knowing they'd done this allowed him to sleep better at night.

She's envious of his relationship with death. Although he doesn't believe in anything comforting – no afterlife, no salvation, no reincarnation – he doesn't seem to be afraid. He feels none of the despair that gnaws away at Rahel at the thought of the end. Feels no horror at the fact that this little, short life is all there is. That there's no return afterwards, no more feeling, just the great void—

Even the slightest thought of it quickens Rahel's pulse. It's not the dying itself that terrifies her, but all those things she hasn't done, hasn't felt, hasn't ventured.

She shakes her head involuntarily, then stops abruptly. A dull pain lingers behind her eyes, and when a moment later she sees Peter turning into the yard with Baila, she walks gingerly towards him, trying to avoid any jolts.

He goes into the stable and emerges straightaway with a bucket. The mare greedily gets to work on its contents – oats, chunks of carrot, two small apples and a handful of wheat pellets. Peter pats and praises the horse as she eats.

"Animals are wonderful."

"Just don't get any ideas about buying one," she says.

He puts a foot against the bucket to stop Baila from pushing it away with her energetic feasting.

"Not in the city . . . But who knows where our future lies. A house in the country like this, with our own well and fire . . ." He looks pensive, then a few seconds later adds, "Imagine the energy supply to the city collapsed. We'd still get by here."

"And if the food ran out," she says sarcastically, "we'd slaughter the horse."

At that very moment Baila lifts the empty bucket with her muzzle and tosses it away. Peter laughs more freely than he has in ages. He throws his head back, puts his hands on his hips and looks years younger.

□

Later, when they're eating in the yard, spraying away the wasps, she thinks of the glint in his eyes when he talked about the house in the country, and at once she realises that such dreams have no attraction for her.

Although she loves summer weeks in the country, she likes the city too. She's far from being fed up with Dresden; she likes her daily walk to work, the little shops, the restaurants and theatres, the excursions and summer evenings drinking wine outside. Peter's cycling trips, on the other hand, are getting longer and he's more and more reluctant to come home.

"I'm worried we're heading in completely different directions," she says, in the hope that he'll disagree.

The one-eared cat slinks around the table and jumps onto Peter's lap, where she curls up elaborately and begins to purr. He smiles and rests a hand on her coat.

□

He sighs. "Sometimes I suppose it can't be helped that two people stop walking in step." His fingers ruffle the cat's fur. "What's so bad about that?"

Rahel is taken aback. "Are you talking about separation?"

"No, Rahel. I'm just thinking out loud."

Her face flushes with heat. "Please think quietly," she hisses.

"There's no need for you to worry," he says calmly. "This place has inspired me to consider a few possibilities. For example, spending the summer as a herdsman on an Alpine pasture."

"You're not thinking in terms of *us* anymore," she says flatly.

"That's not true," he says. "I'm not questioning the *us* at all. At most I'm questioning my role in our relationship. And my career."

The cat leaps off Peter's lap and darts away. As if she had sensed the tension.

Rahel looks at Peter, who seems unusually attractive today. Only seldom does she refer to him as *my husband*. She's always thought of the possessive pronoun as a collar with a chain, but deep down that's exactly the claim she feels: he's her husband and nobody else's. And she's his wife, nobody else's.

Other men of his age have affairs with younger women, become fathers again, buy sports cars or train manically for triathlons. She knows some men who do all of these things at once.

"I'm sorry," she says. "I don't know what's wrong with me."

Don't worry! I love you and want you. These are the sorts of things he would say if he were the hero in a film. But he's Peter and that's why he puts his cutlery to one side, chews thoroughly and says, "A herdsman in the Alps. I like the idea of that."

□

Later in the afternoon she goes on her own to the woods to pick blueberries.

She feels lighter, the headache has gone and within a quarter of an hour she's picked a yoghurt pot of blueberries.

On the way back she comes across a dog. Rahel stops and lowers her head in the hope that it will ignore her. Of course it makes a beeline for her, sniffs her bare legs and drools over them. Its shaggy black fur awakens a memory.

One of her mother's husbands with whom they lived for a while had a similar dog – big and ugly, but well behaved. Rahel was allowed to take him for walks. This didn't particularly appeal to her, but she'd regularly take the dog out just for appearance's sake: a pretty young girl with a huge dog she occasionally told off sharply to accentuate her authority and attract attention, even if he was walking obediently beside her. Her head raised, she'd breeze through the grey streets of Äussere Neustadt, almost car-free in those days, past the run-down houses, in search of other people and the few reflective surfaces she could see herself in with the dog.

Tamara, who'd taken a shine to the dog at first sight, would have loved to go with them, but Rahel always came up with new reasons why she couldn't.

The dog trots into the woods, but the memory of her sister as a child pursues her all the way back to the house.

In Tamara she could see how someone shaped by rejection became the person others saw her as. She'd been born with the corners of her mouth downturned, which made her look grumpy even when she was happy, and at some point grumpiness became her defining feature. She'd stumbled into life like a bird with broken wings.

□

In the kitchen she whips batter for pancakes, adds a handful of blueberries and fries a ladleful in butter. Simon would love this. As a boy he held the record for pancake-eating, easily able to manage half a dozen. Back then she'd never have believed that one day this boy would stand bolt upright, with shorn hair and wearing a perfectly fitting uniform, and swear an oath to the German army.

I promise to faithfully serve the Federal Republic of Germany

and bravely defend the rights and freedom of the German people,
so help me God.

He could have omitted the bit about God, but he uttered it along with the others.

Peter was unexpectedly cheerful throughout the entire ceremony. And although she wasn't happy about Simon's choice, she was glad about Peter's reaction. No frowning or twitching. Not even Simon's appeal to a god Peter didn't believe in drew any sign of displeasure. She loved him for that.

□

Peter puts a rolled-up pancake in his mouth and it's finished in three bites. He immediately takes another.

"You've hardly made these since the children left home," he says as he chews.

"And it's been a long time since I saw you speak with your mouth full," Rahel says, smiling.

He wipes his fingers on a piece of kitchen roll and shrugs apologetically. "They're just too delicious."

Rahel goes outside, leaving him to clear up. The things she's just planted look good. Behind the stables she finds another flowerbed beside the chicken garden, which is so overgrown with weeds she hasn't noticed it before. She almost steps on a plank with rusty nails. She picks it up and leans it against the stable wall, which is cracked in several places. This whole place is a money sink.

In the yard Peter's started feeding the animals. The stork is gulping down defrosted day-old chicks.

"He's prancing around like he's the king of the farm. And he looks so arrogant," she says to Peter, who watches the bird with evident satisfaction. He laughs.

"It's pointless making moral judgments about animals.

They are what they are. Unlike us – we're always pretending to be something."

Rahel rolls her eyes. "I know that. You don't always have to embark on a lecture."

She tries to walk past him but he holds on to her firmly.

"Come here," he says, putting his arm around her and stroking her back.

Rahel leans her head on his chest and closes her eyes. She's almost ashamed to admit it to herself, but it only takes one genuine hug to turn her to jelly.

Friday

Today Rahel waits impatiently for the post.

Over the years it's become more and more difficult for them to get presents for each other. They have everything they need and more. But on Wednesday, after a flash of inspiration, she ordered two gifts for Peter: a Japanese green tea he seldom treats himself to because of the price (almost 60 euros for 100 grams) and a book of photographs of nineteenth-century Dresden.

They're lucky to live in Äussere Neustadt, an area that wasn't totally flattened in February 1945. Peter has read everything about the American and British bombing, especially the air raid on Dresden ordered by Arthur Harris. Once he left an illustrated book on the kitchen table, *Fires: The Bombing of Germany in Pictures.* Simon must have been around ten, and Rahel came into the room too late. He was staring in disbelief at two completely charred bodies, each with one arm raised and the other pointing outwards, and that evening they had an argument about it.

When they go on walks in the city he often tells her how he'd have loved to have seen Dresden before the bombing. The book of photographs is a poor substitute, but hopefully he'll like it.

She wanders down to the mailbox, opens the flap and breathes a sigh of relief. The tea and the book have arrived.

In the late 1990s and early 2000s they would always celebrate Peter's birthday with a group of friends at Saloppe, a summer restaurant close to the Elbe, but neither Saloppe nor their old friends are what they once were.

Or is it the other way around? Have Peter and she changed so much?

For many years their circle of friends was a diverse bunch. The first rifts occurred because of children. Methods of parenting became the subject of intense discussion and some friendships with overly laid-back parents and their children – disagreeable through no fault of their own – did not last.

One of the couples started practising non-violent communication, which meant forsaking irony, amongst other things. To begin with Rahel agreed to go along with it, albeit reluctantly, but Peter delighted in being provocative and gave free rein to his talent. This was another relationship that gradually evaporated.

Other friends insisted that people should declare their political sympathies during a time of rapid social change, something neither Rahel nor Peter were prepared to do. Their views did not sit comfortably in any one political camp. After the incident at the university some of Peter's colleagues disassociated themselves from him too.

New, small, homogenous circles of people formed whose mutual regard was as negligible as their mutual understanding. The more people went on about tolerance, the less of it there was in evidence. That was Rahel's impression, at least. But a few friends did stick by them: Henriette and Axel, both doctors, whose sons are friends with Selma and Simon, and who live nearby in Radeburger Vorstadt; Enzo, the history graduate who runs a second-hand bookshop and lives in a tiny apartment above it; and finally Cordelia, the vintner with her own vineyard near Radebeul. Many years ago Peter got chatting to her at the Elbhang Festival, and once Rahel overcame her jealousy a very close friendship ensued.

As Rahel returns to the house she decides that when they're back in Dresden she'll invite everyone over for a belated party.

□

In her room she moves a chair to the window and calls Ruth.

The first thing she hears is the shrieking of gulls. Right now Ruth is standing barefoot in the sand looking at the sea, she says. It could be the South Pacific today; it's almost turquoise. Stunning.

"Where's Viktor? How's he doing?" Rahel asks.

"He's having some physiotherapy. We went for a little walk on the beach earlier."

"Sounds good!" Rahel says cheerfully, but there's silence on the other end of the line.

"Ruth? Are you still there?"

"Yes, yes." Again there's silence before she asks, "Can you hear that, Rahel? The wind, the waves, the gulls? Sometimes I get up at five o'clock so I can be the first person on the beach. And whenever I see a nice piece of driftwood I pick it up and wonder what Viktor could do with it. We used to always come back from our holidays on the Baltic with boxes of things we'd found, and he'd head straight for his studio, only coming out to eat and sleep." She laughs, though her laughter is without joy.

"Listen, Rahel," Ruth says, "I'm going for a swim now and I'll call again. Maybe not today, but latest on Sunday, Peter's birthday. Bye-bye, my love."

They eat lunch inside because of the heat. Rahel has made tomato, mozzarella and pesto sandwiches, and a green salad on the side. Without asking Peter puts a glass of white wine in front of her. When she eyes it sceptically he says, "Oh, come on. We're on holiday."

After lunch, when they're having coffee, she remembers the cigarette. She hasn't thought about smoking for days, but now she feels the temptation again.

Peter talks and talks. Why isn't he going up to his bedroom, like every other day? He's not giving her any opportunity to slip away. He tells her he's resolved to learn a poem by heart every other day while they're still in Dorotheenfelde. If he begins today he'll know six poems by the time they leave for Dresden. Mental training. Aesthetic fodder for intellectually lean times.

He smiles. "You could do it too."

Rahel shakes her head and pours herself another glass of wine.

"I'm on holiday."

□

Later she stands in the doorway and looks out. There's not a single animal to be seen. Blueish-black clouds darken the sky; the air is shimmering. A gust of wind blows dust past her and she can hear the gentle rumble of thunder in the distance.

Rahel goes up the stairs and stops on the landing. His door is slightly open.

It's pleasantly cool inside Peter's room. Laid out on his bed, hands behind his head and trouser buttons open, he's whispering to himself. Beside him is an open book, face down.

"What are you doing?" she asks, sitting next to him.

"Memorising the first verse of Hölderlin's 'At the Middle of Life'."

"Anyone can do that," she says, sounding unimpressed and, spurred on by the wine, she recites both verses flawlessly.

He looks at her in astonishment, gives a nod of respect and smiles.

Rahel lies down beside him. Nestling her head in the crook of his arm, she places a hand on his tummy. His chest rises and falls rhythmically and she's enveloped by his smell. She closes her eyes and slips a hand inside his trousers.

Surprised by herself she pushes her hand a little further, and when she feels his body react to the movements of her fingers she kisses him. Then his hands reach for her and his stubble scratches her skin. She lets him take off her dress and knickers, and although it's all over after a quarter of an hour she feels as if he's come back to her after a long journey.

Saturday

Shortly after midday they hear the car.

Sipping coffee on the bench beside the front door, they raise their heads in sync and look nervously towards the drive. They're not expecting anyone and the postman must have been already.

Please, no, Rahel thinks. There's a similar concern in Peter's eyes.

Now that the distance between them has diminished, everything from outside is merely a disturbance and a threat.

The car slowly comes into view. A Munich numberplate. Peter's face brightens, Rahel stands up and hurries over.

Selma gets out on the passenger side.

"Hi Mum!" she calls, then opens the back door and lifts out Max, who's asleep.

Simon walks jauntily towards Rahel. His embrace is firm and heartfelt. She breathes in his warm smell and for a moment is transported back to the time when she was still young and he was a baby. She loved the smell of him from day one; she'd soak it up, never able to get enough.

"Well? Are you pleased I brought your little prince?" Selma says, half tongue-in-cheek, half belligerently. Peter puts his arms around her and strokes Max's cheeks, reddened from sleep.

"What are you doing here?" He laughs.

Simon and he embrace firmly too and Selma warbles, "Birthday surprise!"

"But it's not till tomorrow."

"I have to be back in Munich tomorrow evening," Simon says.

Rahel looks at Selma. "Where's Theo?"

"He didn't want to come. I left him with Vince."

Rahel nods and considers this a good sign. Then she puts her hands on Simon's arms and squeezes them. Selma makes a snide noise. "The way she looks at him! It's like she's in love!"

"They haven't seen each other since Christmas, Selma," says Peter to calm the tension, but Rahel immediately shoots him a warning glance.

"Are you hungry?" she says. "I could rustle something up quickly."

Simon shakes his head. "It's fine, Mum. We had something on the way."

There's a hint of a Bavarian accent in his voice.

"Nothing's changed here," he says, looking around. "Time just stands still in this place."

□

Half an hour later Rahel watches her son playing with Max.

Simon is in the water up to his navel. He lifts Max above his head, then suddenly thrusts his arms down, pretending he's going to drop his nephew. Max squeals with delight; he hasn't had enough even after the twentieth time. Simon hands the wriggling little boy back to Selma, but Max leaps towards him again straightaway.

Simon stretches out on the sand. His body is a testament to constant exercise and a healthy livestyle, and Rahel can't help but look at him again and again.

"Was I such hard work when I was a boy?" he asks, grinning and fending off Max who's trying to climb on him from every direction.

Peter's *Yes* and Rahel's *No* come in unison. "No surprise, there," Selma says. "In Mum's memory, only I was hard work."

"You probably were," he replies with a chuckle.

Selma flings a handful of sand at him.

Rahel forces herself to look elsewhere. She'd love a few hours alone with Simon. Conversations with him are a pleasure because he doesn't just come blurting out with things and he never gets himself worked up into a state, as Selma usually does when they talk.

Max is now hanging off Simon's back. He effortlessly manages twenty press-ups before shaking his nephew off, running into the water and diving under. Max starts howling.

The only opportunity to have her son to herself for a while, Rahel thinks, will be early evening when Selma takes Max to bed. She picks up the plastic bag of toys and shakes it out beside Max, and the howling stops as quickly as it began.

Selma has moved over to Peter. Her head is on his shoulder, her hair falling down his back.

"Simon's always so happy," she says sounding reproachful, her heart on her sleeve.

Peter puts his arm around her. "I bet Simon has his difficult moments too. Besides, he hasn't got any children yet. Think back to the time when you—"

"No, it's not that," she interrupts him. "I've never been as happy as him."

Selma snuggles up closer to her father, her torso pressed to her legs, her head drawn in. She stays crouched like this for a long moment.

Then all of a sudden she stands up, skips over to Max, flops down next to him, grabs a shovel and begins to build a sand-castle. All her brooding seems to have vanished at a stroke. She burrows in the sand with childish pleasure, jokes with her son and gives him boisterous kisses.

□

Rahel was never able to play with the children by their rules. Moving toy animals across the parquet floor and talking in silly voices, pretending to be a doll's doctor or a swordfighter, flushing out Simon from his hiding places or dragging a whinnying Selma down the hallway in a cardboard box – all of this bored her senseless, which is why she made it Peter's job. But he hardly proved better in this enforced role.

"Children need to play with children" was his argument each time he stole away. She doubts he's plagued by remorse because of this. Her conscience, on the other hand, is clearly pricked by the sight of Selma's patience with her own child. It whispers words to her like *bad mother, missed opportunities* or *lost and gone for ever*.

She goes to sit beside Peter – in the exact spot where Selma was – and gently strokes his arm. A barely perceptible smile brightens his face. It's only in his eyes and she feels reassured by it.

□

Late in the afternoon, after a substantial refreshment of iced tea, coffee and cake, Peter hauls anxious Max onto the horse and takes him for a walk.

Simon and Selma go to the boulder to send a few mes-sages; Rahel stays sitting where she is for a while.

Vincent's efforts to save his marriage have not been in vain; Selma and he have their first counselling session in a fortnight. Although the idea of studying in Leipzig has not been discounted, the name of the electroacoustic installer hasn't cropped up again. Instead, Selma told them that Vincent could move to the Sächsiche Aufbaubank in Leipzig. A change might do them both good.

Simon, on the other hand, was most evasive in response to questions about his private life. He and Lisa are very busy at the moment, he said. They don't want to define their status, they're keen on being open to change.

"Blah, blah, blah . . ." Selma said, and Simon couldn't help grinning.

Rahel wonders who he's messaging if it's unlikely to be Lisa. None of his girlfriends so far have particularly appealed to her. They're always the same blonde types with ponytails and perfect figures. Selma's theory on this is simplistic but plausible: it's about sex and nothing else.

Selma comes back first. She sits down beside Rahel and sighs.

"Everything OK?" Rahel asks dutifully.

Selma shrugs. "I want to sort things out with Vince, but I don't know how. Whenever he tries to touch me I go rigid. Do you think that'll pass?"

Rahel thinks for a moment, then says, "We had similar problems."

"Really?" Selma's eyes are as wide as saucers. Clearly her daughter didn't expect anything like that between her and Peter. Which means at least they managed to be stable parents to their children.

"It happened from time to time."

"So what did you do?"

"Well," Rahel says. "We were patient. And we had the two of you." She pauses for a moment, then adds, "We never lost interest in each other, never lost the belief that we were right together. Not even in the difficult times. If we hadn't been able to take each other seriously anymore we wouldn't have made it."

Selma's gaze turns inwards.

"Do you still respect Vincent?" Rahel asks, fearful of the answer.

"Yes," Selma says without hesitation.

She sounds as if she's surprised, as if she's never asked herself this question before. Then, out of the blue, she asks, "Have you always been faithful to each other?"

Rahel wasn't expecting this. To lie would be wrong, but she can't saddle her own child with the truth.

The truth is that Peter has never truly stoked her passion. The sex has always been pleasant enough, but never unrestrained. That's why she cheated on him. And having experienced a brief caress that electrified her entire body, a single glance that caused an intense flow of heat in her womb, she knows that the longing for this sensation remains.

"In our hearts, yes," she replies, avoiding eye contact with Selma. She's relieved to see Peter coming into the yard with Max on his shoulders and the horse in tow.

□

At supper Selma casts suspicious glances in Peter's direction.

She must suspect him. Rahel wishes she'd kept her mouth shut.

Peter having an affair. Absurd. But the fact that by his own admission he's never cheated on her in all these years is less an admirable achievement than an expression of his disdain for the sex drive. She knows there have been advances, but they came to nothing. *We're not animals, we can choose* is his credo on this.

Rahel can barely concentrate on the conversation at the

table. She's desperate to set the record straight with Selma, and when later she takes the first opportunity to do so, her daughter stares at her, aghast.

"*You* cheated on *him*?"

Almost threateningly she replies, "Don't you get on your high horse now."

"I wouldn't dream of it," Selma says calmly. Then, after a thoughtful pause, she adds, "Do you think we're like Grandma?"

"No," Rahel answers swiftly and with determination. "We're certainly not like Grandma."

❑

As Rahel had hoped, it takes Selma a while to get Max to sleep, and while Peter is busy in the kitchen Rahel takes the walk with Simon she'd longed for. They don't go far as it's already getting dark. The days are noticeably shorter now.

He tells her he's revising for the entrance examination to be trained as a mountain ranger, that he then wants to train mountain rangers himself, and that he has endless possibilities as a sports scientist if plan A doesn't come off.

What always baffles her is the clarity of his goals. Simon seems to be unaware of the try out, discard and start again attitude which is so common amongst those of his generation, combined with the aspiration for the perfect work–life balance. He doesn't differentiate between work and life.

"Dad's so happy you came," she says, meaning first and foremost herself.

Simon smiles. "I used to dread Dad's birthday because it was also Great-Grandma Anna's and we always had to go to hers for coffee."

The children called her Great-Grandma Airlock because she always sent her husband through "the airlock" when he came home. He had to take off his clothes in the hall, have a wash in the bathroom and put on a clean set of clothes. Only then was he allowed to enter the other rooms. In the sitting room he mostly sat in his brown wingback chair, wrapped in a woollen blanket because Anna always had the windows open. She claimed it smelled of smoke, which it never did. When Ernst died Anna remarked laconically, "At least he's not freezing anymore."

"We had to wash our hands for minutes on end and sometimes she'd brush our hair before we were allowed in," Simon recalls. "And it was cold at hers because the windows were always open."

"Even in winter with the heating on," Rahel adds.

"And that awful room fragrance she sprayed everywhere." He shudders.

"She had severe obsessive–compulsive disorder," Rahel explains, thinking of Edith who'd grown up with this mother and later prevented Anna from having any contact with her granddaughters.

"We're not going to see that wicked lady," Edith told her daughters. "She can't bear children."

Curiously, Ernst never appeared in this story. As if he didn't exist. And yet he was a kind, friendly man who died as he'd lived: quietly, without being a burden to anyone.

□

Later, alone in her room, Selma's question rattles around her head: *Do you think we're like Grandma?* Not even sleep can banish the question; sleep merely pushes it into deeper layers of consciousness where it generates hideous images, from which Rahel wakes at the usual time. No, they're not like Edith, neither Rahel nor Selma.

It's taken her all her life to put together a halfway coherent picture from the fragments she wrested from her mother.

Although born years after the end of the war, Edith was a victim of the conflict. Victim of a mother who'd run through burning Dresden in the Greek goddess costume she'd made herself for Carnival, whose golden shoes got stuck in tarmac molten in the heat and who kept running barefoot until her skin blistered. As she ran she turned to check on her brothers, but behind her was nothing but an ocean of flames.

When, six years later, Anna gave birth to a girl and called her Edith, nobody could see that the horror was still inside her. Edith didn't realise either, but she sensed it throughout her childhood. From then on she was driven through life by the search for this particular feeling, which seemed to exist naturally between others.

Edith didn't know exactly how it felt. Her idea of it was vague and romantic. She sought it in actors, dancers and painters, because at least they were skilled in conveying the feeling. She sought it in other harmed individuals and what she found were alcohol, a colourful life and men who lusted after her, creating the feeling for a brief time, but when it faded she searched again and the only constants in her life were Ruth and Viktor.

But the trauma that plagues all of their lives is ebbing. From generation to generation it loses potency. Even Edith, born into a cold stiffness, wasn't cold and stiff herself. Her love was fickle, but warm. And as for Simon and Selma, the conditions they grew up in were almost ideal.

Rahel closes her eyes and falls asleep soon afterwards. Her dreams now lead her into calmer waters. Edith appears too, but paler than usual, quieter and unusually gentle.

Sunday

The morning light floods brightly through the east-facing kitchen window.

On the table is a bunch of flowers that Rahel has hastily picked. She sees Peter cross the yard with a bucket of chicken feed and calculates that he'll be finished with all the animals in about half an hour. She wished him Happy Birthday as soon as she woke up. After thirteen days she discarded the black linen dress, swapped it for a white shirt dress, and tiptoed barefoot into Peter's room to greet him with a kiss.

Now she sets the table, cracks some eggs and whisks them with a little cream, pepper and salt.

Selma appears with Max on her arm as Rahel's making the coffee.

"Can I have one too? With warm milk, please."

Rahel nods, attends first to brewing Peter's tea, then the milk and finally sits at the table with her daughter.

"Have you got a present for Dad?" she asks.

Selma nods and blows onto her cup.

"Hot," Max says in a serious voice.

"A nice one," Selma says. Then she looks up, holds her boy in a tight embrace and looks Rahel in the eye.

"Mum?"

"Yes, darling?"

"Thanks for staying together, you two. It's nice here, with Dad, Simon and you. It's nice having a family." Her large brown eyes are damp and shimmering, and there's a faint trembling on her lips.

"Oh, darling." Rahel sighs, then leaps out of her chair and puts her arms around Selma's shoulders. She kisses her daughter's forehead and sweeps the hair that's sticking out behind her ears. They laugh and cry at the same time. Max looks up at them in shock, but he seems to sense that everything's OK and sticks his thumb in his mouth.

Simon pokes his head around the door. "Morning, everyone. I'm off for a swim. Back in half an hour."

Selma wipes away her tears. The wave of love takes hold of Rahel's entire body and turns her knees to jelly. She teeters unsteadily back to her chair, but reaches for Selma's hands across the table.

□

After breakfast, Peter unwraps his presents. From Simon and Selma he gets tiny wireless earbuds that he eyes suspiciously.

"I knew he'd have that look," Selma tells Simon, and as if speaking patiently to a child, she explains to her father their advantages. Rahel smiles and doubts he'll ever use them, but when Peter, on the children's insistence, connects the earbuds to his phone and listens to one of his favourite songs – Jeff Buckley's cover of "Hallelujah" – his face lights up and he shouts "Amazing sound quality!", while his entire upper body sways to the surging melody.

"No need to shout!" Selma yells back. Simon slaps his forehead and laughs.

□

After unwrapping the Dresden book he is immediately absorbed by the historical photographs.

Simon and Selma peer over his shoulder.

"Dresden was really beautiful," Selma observes sadly.

"Uh-huh," Peter says, turning the pages. A moment later he stops and says, "And then you have a student sitting in your seminar wearing a T-shirt that says *Bomber Harris do it again.*"

"What?" Rahel looks at him. "You never told me that."

He waves a hand dismissively. "Every word on the subject is a word too many."

"I've seen that as graffiti," Selma says.

Peter shrugs. "A country in which young people call for their own destruction has no future."

"That's just a few idiots," Selma says.

"But idiots that scarcely anyone says boo to. Not even me anymore, by the way."

Simon's head is bowed and his arms are crossed. He's grinding his teeth.

"So I'm serving a country that doesn't have a future," he says tartly. "If it comes down to it, I'll be laying my life on the line for nothing, as far as you're concerned?"

Peter looks up in horror and shuts the book. He sighs and rubs his brow before answering.

"I didn't mean it like that, Simon. But you know how it is."

"Your attitude doesn't make it any better. You could've done something. Called the student out, for example. Asked him if he has any idea what he's telling the world."

"I would have done," Peter says, and having thought for a moment he adds: "I always used to. I explained, argued objectively, made distinctions. But at times like these, cool, sober reflection doesn't stand a chance. All confrontation does is unleash a shitstorm on social media. I'm not up for that anymore. There are more important things in life."

"Such as?" Simon's tone is still gruff.

"You. My family, our friends, good books . . ."

"Oh, I get it," Simon says sarcastically. "So basically you're shirking responsibility?"

"That's enough, now," Rahel butts in. "Your father isn't irresponsible nor is he a coward. You know what happened at the university last year."

At the time she discussed it often with Selma but only once with Simon. She wanted to protect him, prevent him from having any disadvantage on account of his father. In hindsight that seems pathetic, and as if trying to make up for lost time, she now confronts her son with the events of last summer.

In the silence that ensues Peter says, "That's enough! The two of you are only here for a few more hours."

"But not in the kitchen," Rahel says. "I need peace and quiet to bake a cake."

She shoos them all away. On his way out Simon scoops up Max and soon afterwards Rahel sees him through the window, jogging the boy on his knee. Max is squealing with delight.

◻

Later she sits at the kitchen table, one eye on the oven, and the thick, warm, sweet aroma of the rising cake in her nostrils. Selma made it; she's the better baker.

Her daughter stands at the window with her back to Rahel. What she asks is meant to sound casual, but Rahel knows Selma too well to avoid hearing the undertone. Something's not right.

"Could you have the children for the weekend in a fortnight? From Friday to Monday? You can just drop them off at kindergarten on the Monday and I'll pick them up in the afternoon."

"Do you want some time on your own with Vince?" Rahel says, playing the innocent.

Selma doesn't immediately reply. Instead she wanders over to the cooker, bends to peer through the glass window of the oven and says, "Looks good." In a tone of apparent indifference she adds, "Vince is going away for the weekend. Canoe touring on the Unstrut. You know, his annual trip with the lads."

"Look at me," Rahel asks, and when Selma breezes around and tries hard to look her cheerfully in the eye, Rahel knows.

"I thought you wanted to save your marriage."

All the tension in Selma's face now vanishes. With a deep sigh she sits on the chair opposite. "And I do. But I need to work out if my love for Vince is still strong enough."

"And you think that'll be clearer if you spend some time with your lover?"

"Yes!" she says between gritted teeth. "I really do. I mean, maybe I'll realise he's not that great after all."

"On a weekend without children, without obligations and without the routine you're hardly going to see his bad sides, are you, Selma?"

Rahel shakes her head. Her eyes stray outside where Peter and Simon are having a lively discussion while Max sits on the ground, staring spellbound at the stork trudging ponderously across the yard.

"Please, Mum."

"You said earlier how lovely you think it is to have a family."

"Yes! I know. But still . . . How can I put it . . . I'm completely different with . . ." She hesitates to say his name, but then does so, quietly and with great affection. ". . . with Moritz. Somehow I'm more myself."

The day has lost its innocence. Rahel feels a weight descending on her. She senses she's getting smaller, her shoulders slumping forwards, the corners of her mouth sagging.

"Alright," she says wearily. "But I'm not going to lie to your father. This is not a good time for secrets."

"Dad will understand," Selma says confidently, then gives Rahel a kiss on the cheek, grabs her mobile and hurries outside. Rahel sees her sweep past Max and the men towards the boulder. She feels like crying.

She sets a timer so she doesn't forget the cake. Then she goes out into the yard.

Peter is on the phone. By lunchtime all the important people in his life have phoned him. Ruth called very quickly, but promised to phone again tomorrow. Henni and Axel even sang to him, and he invited them for a drink the weekend after next. Rahel can't bring herself to tell him that this is a non-starter because they're going to have the grandchildren.

◻

They spend the rest of the time they have together swimming, walking and eating. There's only a small slice of Selma's excellent cake left; Rahel wraps it in clingfilm and secretly puts it in Simon's bag.

The children set off just after two o'clock. Max will have his afternoon sleep in the car and Simon will get back to Munich before midnight, despite the detour to Dresden.

Curiously, Rahel doesn't feel sorry they're leaving, even though Simon and Selma have been there for only a day. She tries to find some pain inside her, but there's nothing.

◻

At five in the afternoon she opens the bottle of crémant she'd carefully hidden in the fridge and toasts Peter on his fifty-fifth birthday. About an hour later she's lying naked and exhausted beside him in bed. This time he made the first move and now his fingertips are running gently up and down her back.

"I need the loo," she says, but doesn't move. If she lies like this, with her legs bent, she can hold on a while longer.

"It was nice with the children," he says. "But it's also really nice without them."

Rahel turns her head to him in surprise. His fingers are still moving up and down, but now as if automatically, like a machine that won't stop until it's switched off. Then he suddenly takes his hand away and rolls onto his back.

"Do you know what?" he says. "If you took a lover now, I could live with that."

Rahel holds her breath, but Peter keeps talking undeterred.

"I don't think anything can break us apart. We could go our own unconventional ways without losing each other. Don't you think?"

He turns to her but Rahel doesn't move a muscle.

"No," she whispers, "I don't think that's true."

He puts an arm around her, she feels his breath on the back of her neck.

"All I'm saying is that I understand your needs," he says cautiously, and when she asks – still unable to move – about *his* needs, a long pause follows.

"Making love again is nice," he says eventually. "It's just that I would probably be okay with it if we didn't. Either way, I love you."

Those three magical words do not fail to have an effect. Her paralysis gradually subsides and the need to go to the loo returns with such ferocity that Rahel leaps out of bed and straight into the bathroom.

Afterwards she doesn't lie down beside him again.

Peter sits up and runs a hand through his hair. "Sorry. I don't know what got into me just then."

"It's not a good idea," Rahel says, adding after a brief pause, "I think you underestimate the dynamic that another man would bring into our life. Believe me, it doesn't work."

He nods. "Sometimes my mind comes up with ideas—"

"Yes," she says with a sigh. "Sometimes your mind really gets in the way."

Week Three

Monday

The first day of their last week begins with a pain in her left side, which runs down her leg from her bottom like an electric shock. Rahel's sciatic nerve has often put her out of action. She rolls out the yoga mat and does the exercises her physiotherapist showed her for when this happens. Twisting the spinal column and a few specific stretches bring relief, but when the jet of water later hits the hollow of her knee in the shower, she winces again.

She shakes a spider off the towel and watches it scurry away, not for the first time. She wonders if it's always the same spider. Then she dries herself, puts on some jeans and a colourful tunic, and goes carefully down the stairs.

The fact that with each passing year her body is behaving more like a moody diva casts a cloud over her view of the future. But Rahel has resolved not to let bones, vertebrae, tendons, muscles and nerves control her life. Sometimes she even talks to the culprit of the moment, and today it's the turn of her sciatic nerve. If it leaves her alone, she promises to nurture its wellbeing with daily exercises.

□

Peter's sitting outside in the yard, surrounded by cats and totally absorbed by the pilgrim book. He must have glimpsed her out of the corner of his eye because, without looking up, he shifts to the side and pats the space beside him.

"Viktor wrote something in here," he says.

"Really? What?"

"*I wish I could believe.*"

"So do I," Rahel says with a sigh. "And I know what you're thinking."

When the children were small a sudden onset of fear made Rahel toy with the idea of having them christened. "Our children are not joining that organisation," Peter had said categorically.

He seldom came out with such an intransigent *No!*, but whenever he did, Rahel didn't stand a chance. And in this instance she had no sound reason apart from the fact that the christening would reassure her.

His *No!* both annoyed and relieved her. How could she have given the children an everyday religious upbringing? They were the third godless generation.

Peter nudges her in the side.

"So it's that time again, is it?" he teases her.

She laughs and gives a shrug.

"Belief is a source of strength that I don't possess."

"Find a different one," he replies impassively. The one-eared cat comes up, jumps onto his lap, turns around and curls into a ball.

"If only it were so simple . . ."

Again the pain shoots down her leg. She puts her left foot on her right thigh and presses her hands gently onto the bent left leg.

"Sciatic nerve?" he asks, concerned.

"How do you know?"

"Because you always do that when it hurts."

"I'm getting old."

Without responding to that he asks, "How about we drive to Ahrenshoop for the day and visit Viktor and Ruth?"

"I've already thought of that," she says, shifting her weight onto her right buttock before standing up. "But like this I won't be able to sit in the car for hours."

She paces up and down a few times, then rests her left leg on the bench.

Peter fondles the purring cat's remaining ear. He prods it with his fingertip and smiles when the cat flinches.

"If Viktor's up to it, will you speak to him?" he says. Then after a pause he adds, "If he really is your father you'll inherit this house one day."

Rahel stays in the pain-relieving leg-up position.

"I've already thought of that too," she concedes.

Slowly she brings down her leg, kneels, stretches again and breathes a sigh of relief. Either the pills are taking effect or the stretching has helped – at any rate a twinge is all that's left of the pain.

◻

Peter comes with her to the lake even though he had a swim before breakfast.

"What were you and Simon talking about yesterday? When you were standing in the yard?" she asks on their way to the swimming spot.

"The state of the nation," he replies with a clearly ironic undertone, but then adds in all seriousness that they were discussing the respect Simon might get, or more likely not get as a career soldier. Public opinion on the military had fundamentally changed. Was he aware of the life he would lead? Frequent transfers, tours abroad, genuine danger, not to mention rejection by those who regard soldiers as murderers.

"And?"

Peter shrugs. "He's going to do it anyway. *Someone has to do it*, he said. *So that the rest can live in their colourful bubbles.* And he's right."

They'd actually decided not to stick their oar in anymore. *If nobody's prepared to defend the conditions necessary for freedom, then that's the end of freedom*, Simon once said, and although she agrees with him, she's still reluctant to see her own son assume this responsibility.

She sighs.

"But for this country!" Peter says loudly. "With its prohibitions, rules and regulations down to the minutest detail. This country that has no regard for genuine freedom—"

"Peter," Rahel says, grabbing his arm. "Don't."

He takes a deep breath and simply nods.

□

At their swimming spot an elderly woman in a sporty bathing suit is sitting up against a tree, gazing out over the lake. She turns to them, says hello, gathers her things and makes to leave.

"We don't mean to drive you away," Peter says, but she assures them she has to go home anyway.

As Rahel cautiously tries a few strokes so as not to aggravate the nerve, she's no longer thinking about Simon, but about next week. Around this time next Monday, sitting opposite her will be Jannik B., a weepy twenty-five-year-old. He lacks all intrinsic motivation. Every other sentence begins, "It's my right . . ." A pitiful individual with the maturity of a small child.

It took Rahel many hours to find out what had gone wrong in his sheltered life. One day he told her about the reward system his parents used throughout his childhood. For each good school grade he got money, likewise for taking out the rubbish, emptying the dishwasher or going shopping. Every task done voluntarily received lavish praise and he couldn't recall ever being criticised by his parents. The rewards increased as he got older, assuming remarkable dimensions. The self-image that emerged from this upbringing has collided with a world that doesn't afford him the same degree of attention and admiration.

□

Susanne L. will come in straight afterwards, a thirty-eight-year-old who recently had her first child. She wanted a home birth but had to go to hospital at the last minute. Now the dominant emotion in her life is not joy at her perfectly healthy baby, who was saved from a dangerous lack of oxygen by a Caesarean section, but the sense that she's been traumatised by the forceful intervention. She and her husband wanted it to happen very differently – with lovely music, being conscious of the experience, and of course without hospital staff. In their first session Rahel couldn't refrain from saying that Frau L. had these people to thank for the fact that her child was alive. Nonetheless the woman insists on her suffering. A trauma whose origin lies in the discrepancy between what she wished for and the reality.

□

Then, after a coffee break, Rahel will see thirty-one-year-old Hannes F., who ever since his excessive marijuana consumption as a teenager has been suffering from psychoses, has never held a job down for longer than a few months, prefers to spend his time chilling, and only ever talks about one thing:

149

universal basic income. If he received that he'd realise all manner of projects, and if Rahel then asked him why he didn't just get on with them, he'd reply that the agency was breathing down his neck and he had enough to do trying to get out of the jobs offered to him. All beneath his level he'd say with a shake of the head. Asking too much of him mentally.

□

Comfortable times produce weak people, she thinks, without excepting herself.

The patience she has for her clients has diminished substantially. It's high time she had a supervision; she'll arrange an appointment as soon as they're back from holiday.

Rahel puts her head under water, abandons herself to the weightlessness and lets thoughts of work go. They float away and even the pain has dissipated; the moment is perfect. She surfaces again, looks at the shore where Peter is standing with his trousers rolled up, and wishes she could always return to this moment.

□

Ruth's call comes late in the afternoon. Viktor is considerably better, she says cheerfully – a real leap in his recovery. She can't explain it, but this morning he talked about the future for the first time, and surely that must be a sign that he was bucking up. There hadn't been much progress with his fine motor skills, so any creative work was out of the question, but his speech was getting better, they were lengthening the walk and his appetite was growing by the day. He was beginning to be like his old self again too. That morning when an assistant treated him like a little child he said harshly that he might be old but he wasn't an idiot. And he cracked a joke over lunch too.

"Oh, Ruth," Rahel says, "I'm so pleased."

Peter, who's standing at the foot of the stairs with his arms crossed, smiles and gives Rahel the thumbs up. Then she asks Ruth, "How about if we came to visit you? On Thursday, for example."

Ruth says nothing for a moment.

"Visit?" she repeats eventually. "Why not? But I'll have to ask Viktor first. It might be too much for him."

It's never been possible to make an arrangement with just one of them; it's always been *I'll have to ask Viktor*, or *Let's see what Ruth says*.

How many decisions has she made without consulting Peter? How often has he only found out in the afternoon that they've got guests coming to dinner that evening? How often has she chosen their holiday destination, bought furniture or brought in decorators?

When Ruth hangs up, Rahel takes a few steps towards Peter.

"Have you ever thought I'm too dominant?"

He laughs out loud. "Let's just say your decisions have always been more like decrees."

"But you've never told me that!" she says, feeling tension building within her.

"*Aye, aye, Cap'n* or *Yes, Madam!* or *At your command, General* obviously weren't clear enough."

As he's saying this her tension escalates into a sudden fury. His whole manner now comes across as patronising. His act of superiority, his arrogantly subtle remarks. What is he thinking?

"What's wrong?" he asks, and the innocence in his voice really irritates her.

"What should be wrong?" she hisses. "Apart from the fact

151

that I'm to blame, of course! You had to suffer because I ignored your hints wrapped in irony."

"I never said I suffered. You were the one who brought this up!" He looks at her in confusion. "It's not easy to criticise you. You can be quite intimidating. I don't know if you're aware of that."

He ought not to have uttered those words. It's as if he's opened all the floodgates and is now submerged by a torrent of stored-up anger. Because of all those days he's excluded her, all those hours of his hurtful self-reliance and because of the tame sex that never sated her appetite. Her will is powerless here. For she certainly didn't want this to happen; she wasn't even aware it was. As the words come cascading out, she's horrified by their ferocity and when finally everything has been said, she stands facing him, exhausted.

"Oh God, I'm sorry, I'm so, so sorry."

But instead of being angry, he says charitably, "At some point you boil over. At some point it just happens, doesn't it? I understand that."

"No!" she yells. "You don't understand at all. You *never* boil over!"

"You're mistaken there, Rahel," he counters sharply. "You've no idea what goes on inside here," he adds, tapping his head.

Then he leaves.

In typical Peter fashion, without saying another word.

□

Later she stands outside the door to his room, hoping he might sense her presence. Didn't he hear her coming? The floorboards creak with every step; even shifting weight from one foot to the other makes a sound. As she listens carefully she thinks back to something Peter said in spring. Because of the virus, people were beginning to give each other a wide berth. She was one of those who people made room for, whereas he was someone who gave others the right of way. When they were hiking in the mountains on narrow paths, he said, Rahel would always stay on the path; those coming the other way would squeeze themselves against rocks or climb up the hill a little to make way for her.

"You just slot into life," he said. "You're such a natural in this world, whereas I . . ." He didn't finish his sentence.

She didn't think any more of this at the time, but now she feels these words are like the key to the door behind which his inner nature is revealed.

It sounds so quiet in there.

She touches the handle, hesitates, takes her hand away again, then walks briskly down the landing to her room.

Tuesday

The hand on her shoulder is cool and the aroma of freshly brewed coffee tickles her nostrils.

"It's only me," Peter whispers.

"What time is it?" she mumbles.

"Just after seven." He takes his hand away and clears his throat.

"You were standing outside my room yesterday," he says. "I heard you. I wanted to get up, open the door and talk to you. I really did. But I couldn't. My whole body felt paralysed."

She sits up, takes out her night guard and reaches for the coffee cup he's holding out to her.

"Sometimes my loneliness is so great . . ." His arms rise, his hands grab at thin air and then he lowers them again. "Whenever I want to talk to you about it, I can't find the words. Or I find them but can't say them."

For a moment he just stares out of the window.

"Only seldom do I get the feeling that you really understand me, Rahel. Maybe all your patience is used up on your clients." He gives a bitter laugh. "You ought to have married an optimist. Some jolly mover and shaker."

She hates it when he says things like this. After almost thirty years together she doesn't want to hear him say that her life has been a mistake.

"Stop it, Peter," she says in a curt voice, but then adds more gently, "I'm not asking you to become someone else."

He gives her a weary smile, and for a split second, as in a time-lapse image, she can see the old man he's going to be.

"I love you," she says. "And I want us to be together."

Leaning her head on his back, Rahel puts her arms around Peter and holds him tight. Then she gets up, goes to the loo, and when she returns he's lying in her bed.

His eyes are closed and his breathing is regular. "I'm not asleep," he says.

She kisses his forehead and goes quietly out of the room.

◻

As she nibbles her toast without relish she writes a shopping list.

The mere thought of it drains her of energy. The less she does, the feebler she seems to become. For the first time since the beginning of the holiday she's missing the tight rhythm of daily life, that virtuous feeling of being tired in the evening, having managed to juggle a hundred different things in the day. For her, a life without obligations holds little charm.

She folds the piece of paper, peers out into the yard and is assailed by a memory.

She must have been about eight. Edith, Tamara and she had gone to Dorotheenfelde over New Year, and a severe snowstorm struck. It kept up for days and they were cut off from the outside world by snowdrifts, several metres high, around the house and yard.

Viktor and a second man – one of the other families still lived in the house back then – cleared the area around the front door with shovels and soon there was a mound of snow towering in the yard. It was bitterly cold and neither Rahel nor

Tamara were kitted out for such weather. Tamara was sat on a fur in front of the stove with her toys, but Rahel was keen to go outside. With the help of the two men she dug a path through the mound of snow in the yard, which they expanded into a cave in the middle. In no time Rahel's woollen gloves were wet and frozen stiff, the wind whistled through her hat and the cold hurt her ears. But at some point she was sitting inside the mound of snow and it was silent. The sort of silence that only comes with snow. The storm had died down and, when Rahel crawled out the other side of the cave, the few snowflakes that were still falling glistened silvery in the sun. Blinded by the blazing light, the beauty and the winter silence, she just sat there for ages. Finally, someone (Viktor?) picked her up and took her into the kitchen, where she was undressed and her numb feet put in a tub of cold water until they began to tingle and hurt; and someone (Ruth?) peeled an orange and forked the pieces into her mouth. As she ate the sweet orange Rahel cried with pain and the grown-ups argued about who'd left her outside. It ended with Edith running out of the kitchen in tears, which is what she always did when things got too much for her. She never finished a difficult conversation; sooner or later she'd cry, "It's fine. I'm to blame! Who else?"

The memories come at will. On this summer's day, after more than forty years, Rahel can see her mother's tears, taste the orange and feel her half-frozen feet. She's choked by sadness that she never recognised her father in Viktor at the time, and if there had still been any doubt as to whether she ought to probe further, that has now gone.

□

Rahel takes two empty shopping bags, goes out to the car and feels as if she's just a few metres from a goal. Soon she will come face to face with Viktor. Then she'll know. Even if he doesn't give her an answer she'll see it in his eyes.

□

Just beyond the boulder her phone rings. She stops the car.

"Hi!" Selma says, almost affectionately. "I just wanted to check whether next weekend works."

Rahel rolls her eyes. That explains it.

"I haven't talked to your father yet."

"Why not?"

"It just hasn't come up. We've had our own things to talk about here," she says.

Rahel hears a crashing and clattering in the background.

"Max bumped into the cupboard on his balancing bike," Selma says calmly.

"And what's Theo up to?"

"Good question." Rahel hears Selma call Theo's name, then it goes silent for a few seconds.

"Mum? Are you still there?"

"Yes, yes," Rahel replies impatiently.

"Theo's been cutting his hair. I've got to hang up. But let me know when you've spoken to Dad."

□

She drives slowly down the road to the village. One of her top teeth is making its presence felt. She's noticed it for several days. It's not toothache; she can just feel that it's there. This sensation is an announcement. Sooner or later the pain will come.

The baker's van is in the village today. It's parked outside the former Konsum shop.

When she was a child her stomach used to tingle as she

climbed the three steps to the shop. The range of goods here always seemed much bigger than in Dresden. Perhaps she was mistaken, perhaps it was just that Viktor bought her whatever she wanted.

Rahel parks the car and joins the end of the queue. The old women are chatting away in the regional accent. They're complaining about the chancellor and the drought, they lift their masks and state that life was no better in the past, but less crazy. Rahel listens to them in such amusement that the queue almost moves too fast for her.

As she drives on into town, her tongue keeps straying to the tooth, pressing it, feeling it, trying to appease and calm it; it's as if the tooth has woken up and is now demanding attention. The memory of the agony she's felt during nights of toothache sends a shiver down her spine. Without realising it, she accelerates.

At the grocery she fills the trolley with enough to last them till the end of their stay, and so that there are some supplies for whoever comes after them.

Only four more days.

A young woman queuing at the till is on the phone, prattling away loudly and cheerfully about her depression. Her outward appearance might suggest otherwise – make-up, lipstick, mascara and hairdo all immaculate – but it's not for nothing that standards have changed. The ICD-10 catalogue, the international classification of mental and behavioural disorders, has been refined over the years. Whereas at the beginning of Rahel's career a few weeks of melancholy was seen as completely normal, a temporary rough patch, now it's classified under the affective disorders F32.0, F32.1 and F32.2 – the various manifestations of depression. Anyone whose symptoms last longer than two weeks can be categorised as ill.

Sometimes she wonders whether all of psychology isn't just a huge mistake – an evaluation of perfectly normal states of mind in keeping with the spirit of the time. A permanent overinterpretation. Supposedly a quarter of all children have behavioural problems. If that's the case, they'll all be sliding into a social catastrophe.

Rahel seldom says this sort of stuff out loud. Not for fear of causing offence, but because the more she utters it the more truth it assumes. She even avoids discussing the topic with Peter, worried that he'd agree with her and only reinforce her doubts. Because, despite everything, she loves her job and she knows from her clients that she can often be of real help.

When her shopping has been scanned she hands over two hundred-euro notes, at which the cashier tuts and mutters, but Rahel wishes her a good day all the same. From an ice-cream van in the car park she buys a chocolate and vanilla soft ice, then sits in the driver's seat of her car with the door open.

The tooth doesn't react to the cold.

□

On a late walk through the fields Peter reaches for her hand. Baila is trotting behind them, but sticking obstinately to Peter's side.

The rolling hills of the Uckermark undulate all the way to the horizon. The wheat is ripe, the sky broad. Above them a red kite circles; Rahel thinks it's a buzzard. Peter hands her the binoculars.

"Fair enough," she concedes when the bird arcs and she sees the deeply forked, reddish tail.

"There's so much I could get my teeth into. Like ornithology," he says chirpily. "Everything is more fun than what awaits me at the university."

"Maybe you'll get lucky and the virus will come to your rescue."

A mischievous smile brightens his face.

Then she tells him about the old women at the baker's van and how they didn't think the old days were better, just less crazy. She knows he likes hearing this and immediately he translates it into his own language. "There aren't facts any longer, only constructs. This baffles people. They sense it isn't right, but they keep hearing it again and again. So long and so often that they no longer trust their own instincts."

Rahel smiles. "The old women still trust their instincts," she remarks.

"But the old women will soon be dead," Peter points out.

□

It's dark by the time Ruth calls. She sounds a little tipsy and admits they've almost finished the second bottle of wine, she and Frauke, the friend she's staying with. She's feeling fantastic, she tells Rahel; she spent a wonderful day by the sea with Viktor, in a canopied wicker beach chair with a picnic.

"You won't believe this," she says excitedly. "He wanted to go for a swim!" Ruth was barely able to stop him. When she mentioned their visit he looked like a startled deer, she says, laughing. "But do come up and see us. Thursday would be best."

□

Peter is still sitting at his desk.

Viewed from behind, in the wan light of the small lamp, he suddenly looks like an old man.

"Ruth called," she says softly. "We can go up on Thursday."

"Fine."

160

He turns to her, takes off his glasses and is young again. "Come here," he says.

He lifts her onto his lap – her petite, light body – puts his arms around her waist, buries his head in her breasts and makes a cosy sound like a contented child. Rahel stiffens at once. She can't bear sentimental men. Sensitive, tender, yes. But this? She's not his mother.

Rahel pushes herself away. Claiming to need the loo, she hurries out of his room.

Later she comes back. He's already in bed, and his detached look tells her that he's understood.

"I'm sorry," she lies. "I'm feeling tense. My tooth."

Pointing to her left cheek she pulls a face. Then she lies down beside him, curls up and buries herself in his embrace.

All the things he doesn't know about her.

That sometimes she dances around their apartment, singing to loud music.

That she has fantasies. Unmentionable ones.

That she prays in secret.

That she's worried about losing him.

That she fears she'll be responsible.

That she would never claim to be wholly trustworthy.

That she'd have a better conscience if he felt the same way.

"Hold me tight," she says.

He does so and kisses her hair. She feels calm inside again.

Wednesday

Just before three in the morning Rahel rushes into the bathroom, feeling dizzy and bathed in sweat. Afterwards she sits shivering in bed for a good hour, waiting for the painkillers to take effect. She slips into a doze, from which she wakes with a start every half hour. Shortly after half past six she drags herself to the loo, and later creeps into Peter's room to tell him she's heading into town to see a dentist.

◻

The dentist's muscle tone suggests she's a sportswoman. Every movement is right. Rahel immediately relaxes a little and entrusts herself to this woman's care.

A tiny wad of cotton wool is dampened with freeze spray and pressed against Rahel's tooth.

Nothing.

"Vitality test negative," the dentist says to her assistant.

Rahel is given an X-ray and has to wait.

Back in the treatment room the news comes as no surprise: the root is inflamed. But root-canal treatment would be difficult, because the tooth has three long, severely crooked roots. It's unlikely they'd be able to keep it quiet on a long-term basis.

An hour or so later, after Rahel has filled out and signed

every form under the sun, declaring that she won't drive after the surgery, she leaves the practice with a thick, blood-soaked swab in her mouth. She keeps biting on it for a while, then spits it into a tissue and drives off.

□

Peter is waiting for her with a concerned look on his face. He brings her a cold pack that he's wrapped in a clean dishcloth, sits on her bed and strokes her arm.

"It's OK," she mumbles. "I'll be better by this evening."

But his expression remains serious.

"I've got some bad news," he says. "While you were away the phone kept ringing. I didn't answer at first because I didn't think it would be for us, but then . . ." He pauses for a moment. "Viktor's gone missing."

"What?"

"He must've left the rehab clinic very early, before the morning shift change. There's been no trace of him since."

Rahel reaches feebly for her phone which she'd put on silent during her treatment. Three missed calls from Ruth.

"Ruth fears the worst," Peter says. "Viktor didn't leave a suicide note, but he can't write anymore. They've notified the police and the coastguard. If he went into the sea there's very little hope. Since yesterday there've been high waves with a strong undercurrent. Even a good swimmer—"

"No," she whispers. "It's not possible."

She looks at Peter.

"There's nothing we can do," he says.

□

She feels as if she's trapped in water. There's a rushing in her ears. The sea, she thinks – that's what the sea sounds like.

But then the rushing becomes a roaring and she's gripped by a fierce giddiness. Peter gets the bucket to her in time. She throws up in a single burst, then sinks back onto the bed. Peter hands her a flannel and takes the bucket away.

The anaesthetic is still working on the left side of her face; the numbness extends all the way behind her eye. But gradually the pain from the surgery stirs, mingling with that other pain that no tablet can deal with.

On the bedside table is the elf with the broken wing. Rahel picks it up, strokes the spot where it's broken and prays quietly.

□

She spends the following couple of hours in a helpless state of hope. The telephone is beside her and when a text arrives from Selma asking yet again about the coming weekend, Rahel doesn't reply.

She sees Viktor before her, sitting and carving by the shore of the lake on an autumn day. His hands move with supple assurance and he's humming a song.

Which song?

Closing her eyes, she summons the memory, but the sounds merge into one, then the image blurs and is replaced by a different one.

Edith after her cancer had returned. Edith in her noisy suffering.

She's smoking, coughing and prowling like a caged animal around their little apartment. Her furious railing against fate begins with her mother, Anna. Then her father gets a dressing-down because he suffered in silence. Then men in general, followed by capitalism, the plunderers from the West and finally Viktor. But what exactly did she say?

Later, as she died courageously, there were no more such

outbursts. She passed the final test with flying colours. Viktor came once too, but didn't stay long. Did the two of them talk alone, was Ruth there? Rahel can't remember.

There's too much she doesn't know.

If she'd had time with Viktor she would have asked him about it.

She realises to her horror that she's already assuming he's dead, and when the phone rings she's expecting confirmation.

It's Frauke. There's no news, the search is ongoing and Ruth has gone for a lie-down.

□

Early in the afternoon Rahel pulls herself together and freshens up. Her face is barely swollen. She looks better than she feels.

She swallows a painkiller prophylactically, goes down the stairs and finds Peter in the yard.

"Heard anything yet?"

She raises her arms helplessly. "They're still searching."

"Selma called," he says. "She's asking if we could take the children next weekend. Apparently you knew about this?"

Incapable right now of filling him in with the background, she merely groans.

Peter puts an arm around her and gently pulls her towards him. "We'll get through all this," he whispers.

This is the man she loves. Who doesn't demand words from her when she doesn't have any. Who knows the right thing to do at this moment. Closing her eyes, she gives herself up to his embrace and tells herself Viktor has just gone on a long walk.

□

The news comes during supper.

It's Ruth herself on the phone. Her voice doesn't quaver in the slightest as she gives a brief summary of events. The coastguard found Viktor a few hours ago. His body had drifted far out to sea; he must have swum a fair way before drowning. Nobody can explain it.

She's already identified the body and is now back at Frauke's. There are a few things to sort out but she'll probably come home on Saturday.

When Rahel asks if it would be any help if she and Peter drove to Ahrenshoop, Ruth answers with a terse and resolute No. More gently she adds, "You'll be most help to me if you keep everything in order in Dorotheenfelde."

"Of course," Rahel says. She then falls silent because anything else would end in a sob.

"Bye-bye, Rahel," Ruth says, and hangs up.

□

Peter stays in her room that night.

She lies fatigued beside her husband, listening to him talk. He must have had such determination to do that, Peter says. The courage he must have had to wander into the dark water.

She wonders how cowardly you have to be not to tell your own child that they're your child. But maybe none of that is true, maybe her thoughts are being obscured by her longing.

Father or not – the loss affects her deeply. Soon there will be nobody left ahead of them. Neither of Peter's parents are still alive, Edith has been dead for eleven years and now Viktor. After Ruth, she and Peter will be next in line; it's pointless to complain about it.

All of them will be vanquished eventually.

Thursday

She slept a little.

Where yesterday there was still a tooth she can feel the stitches but no more blood and no pain.

Peter is already up. She could sense it without opening her eyes, merely by feeling the cool draught on her arms and neck.

A glance out of the window tells her it must still be early. In the pale, shadowless light she sits up and thinks of Ruth. How will she be able to cope with everything here? She's still spry and healthy, but the house, the animals and the huge amount of land are too much for one person. She's going to have to sell up.

It's got to that stage, Rahel thinks. From here on in the losses outweigh the gains. Reluctantly she shakes her head, gets up, staggers over to the bathroom and rinses her mouth out with water. Then she puts on some clothes and goes downstairs into the kitchen.

◻

After breakfast she tells the children. Simon answers after the second ring. He says what people say when things like this happen, and Rahel knows that Viktor's death won't change anything about how his day pans out.

She talks longer to Selma, who says kind, clever things

about Viktor, especially about his work. Then she cries and her daughter's sobbing does Rahel good. In grief she suddenly feels close to Selma.

Years ago she once told her, "I hope you have a daughter who's just like you."

The hope had been a curse, a furious malediction.

Were she to repeat those words today, she would mean it differently.

Before Rahel hangs up after several seconds of silence, she tells her daughter she loves her.

The exhaustion has now spread to her fingertips. She puts her face in her hands and waits for Peter, waits to feel better, but all that comes are new tears and an impotence. Besides Viktor's death, she's crying for all those words she's hurt Selma with.

□

What on earth should she do today?

When Peter comes in and asks if there's anything he can do for her, she says no.

Then, in the doorway, he says, "I'm almost happy it's behind me."

"What are you talking about?"

"The death of my parents."

She nods and wipes away the tears.

After many years of being addicted to sleeping pills and anti-depressants, Peter's mother died early – at seventy – of dementia in a home. By then his father had been dead for a few years. Severely overweight, he didn't survive the heart attack he suffered shortly after retiring.

Peter's relationship with his parents was distanced. He'd estranged them through his education. Although they were more proud than anything, they were no longer able to relate to him. They just called their son *the Professor*.

His parents would endlessly go on about their lost homelands: East Prussia in the father's case, Lower Silesia for the mother. But no matter how often Peter suggested it, they refused to visit the places of their childhood with him. After their deaths Peter went alone to explore his and their roots, having first researched it all thoroughly.

What can Rahel research? She doesn't even know if she should mourn Viktor as a friend or as his biological daughter.

On Edith's side, her mother Anna had been the only surviving member of the family. Anna's mother and her brothers died in the bombing of Dresden; her father, a lawyer, died in Russian captivity. Anna escaped with nothing but the clothes on her back. Everything that could have been testament to the existence of her family was burned to a cinder on the night of the bombing. Later, she took the first man she found from the few available, had a daughter and became a teacher.

If there was anything at all that had remained of the family's devastated middle-class life, it was an air of confidence that Anna occasionally showed, which Edith is said to have had too, and which Peter sometimes fancies he sees in Rahel.

□

Neither of them did enough research. They didn't ask enough questions while they were still able. They were too preoccupied by the change of system, relearning, learning in general, earning money, bringing up children, travelling and becoming Western, fitting in. Then the pausing, hesitating, refusing and reverting to their own ways of thinking, their own experience. But when their identities had been sharpened and consolidated, and they were ready to ask the obvious questions of those closest to them, the respondees were dead. Despite the difference in their ages, they passed away in quick succession after the turn of the millennium. Edith outlived her mother by a paltry year.

□

Making use of her first hint of energy, Rahel hastens to the studio. She heads straight for the cabinet, opens the drawer with the sketches of Edith and herself, and takes out the entire contents. She opens more drawers, grabbing anything that seems to be connected to her life. She slaps sheets of paper on the pile – drawings, etchings, sketches – and puts the pilgrim book on top.

She scans the entire studio.

That wooden sculpture over there – doesn't it have her mother's features? And the girl made of burr wood at the back – isn't that her face?

Now her eyes take in everything. As if she'd only just learned to truly see.

She feels like destroying it all. Scribbling furiously over the fine drawings in thick red pen and cutting deep notches in the wooden sculptures.

If Peter hadn't come she would have got even with Viktor.

□

He takes her out into the yard.

The way he looks and talks at her makes Rahel angry. As if she were a deranged child.

"I'm fine," she rebuffs him. "You don't have to worry."

Unconvinced, he stays close beside her.

"I'm just livid," she hisses. "How could Viktor be so easy about it?"

"I don't think it was easy for him." He sighs and kneads his hands. "But whatever you do, you mustn't tamper with his work, Rahel."

A few tears run down her cheeks. She wipes them away, takes a deep breath and thinks of the headache she gets when she really starts to cry.

"I know that," she says defiantly.

He hands her a tissue. Blowing her nose, she says, "I'm going to take the drawings of my mother and me."

He takes her hand and strokes it.

"No!" she barks harshly, but then apologises at once.

"It's fine."

Something spiteful is stirring inside her. She wants to hit him round the head with his reason, but without his level-headedness and his kind face she'd be lost right now.

They go their separate ways – Peter back into the house, Rahel into the studio. She takes the pile of drawings, as well as the book, the tobacco and rolled cigarette, and carries it all up to her room.

□

When she drives to the village with Peter in the afternoon it's turned a little cooler. She's wearing a light cardigan and is happy just to be going along for the ride rather than having to make decisions.

At the fishmonger's Peter buys some supplies for the stork, smoked trout for Rahel and eel for himself. She waits in the car, her head resting against the window.

Have you heard? Viktor's dead! she thinks.

How often must he have cycled to the village, had a chat, enquired about fish stocks in the nearby lakes and railed against the eco-Berliners who'd moved here? He could be jovial if he felt like it. And he would talk to anyone. He made no distinction between classes, money or no money, education or not. He didn't care a jot.

Viktor is dead.

He could be coarse if he wanted. And he was certainly blunt. His views on art were crystal clear, and his judgment was occasionally withering because he had the knowledge and conviction to pass it. He'd never have begun his working day with the words *I feel motivated*. He would have cracked up at anyone who talked like that.

Viktor is dead.

He could drink a lot and talk big, love intensely, laugh loudly and put people's noses out of joint. Not because he was malicious, but because he loved freedom. What was bad he called bad, and what was good good, and he never said *as it were*.

Viktor is dead. She didn't know how hard it would hit her.

Peter puts the shopping on the back seat and they drive off. He turns at the crooked cul-de-sac sign, then it's along the track, up the hill and past the boulder into the yard.

Her heart feels heavy.

The stork is standing by the front door as if he were the new master.

Friday

As dawn is breaking she is overcome by sleep.

It's almost eleven o'clock when she opens her eyes again. Still dozing, she briefly thought it had all been just a bad dream. These are the worst moments. When the horror of reality exceeds the horror of the night.

Peter is doing his best. He's not saying too much or too little. He's just there, taking her on his stroll with the horse.

As they walk it occurs to her how like Viktor he is. Like a gentler version of him, without the sharp edges but with the same inner intransigence towards anything he considers to be wrong. The keep-all-options-open doesn't suit him. Just like Viktor, he closes the door on hypocrites and frauds.

"Let me know if you want me to shut up," he says, but listening to him feels good.

He lay awake in the night too, thinking about life and death.

"Everything we do, every tiny action forms our lives and personalities. If I'm too sedentary I get ill, whereas if I exercise I feel better. If I read bad books the bad works its way into me and then out of me. If I read good books, the good works its way into me and out of me. If I lie, I warp something inside me. If I tell the truth I straighten it out again."

She looks at him. "Sounds like our destiny is in our hands."

"No, that's not what I mean. I know there's not much that we determine. We do not come into the world unconditioned."

Rahel nods. "One of the biggest fallacies of our time: everyone can determine who they are. Every person a little god. As if there were nothing set in place. As if there were no before."

With the *before* she's back to Viktor. It doesn't matter what they talk about, all words lead back to him.

□

Selma calls in the early evening.

"How are you, Mum?" she asks, sounding genuinely concerned.

Rahel says what she can, plays it down, pretends to be stronger than she is. She does what parents do.

Then, as if it weren't important, Selma mentions the coming weekend. It's sorted, she says.

"What happened?"

"Erm." Selma sniffs and blows her nose. "I told Moritz what had happened. That you don't know how things are going to pan out. Stuff like when the funeral is, whether Ruth needs help. I said I didn't know if you could take the kids."

"And?"

"He was upset." Her voice goes very high. "*He* was upset. Because I hadn't made it possible to see him."

"A narcissist," Rahel says soberly. "Overblown sense of entitlement. Easily offended."

"You said it."

"So, what now?"

"If you had the time," Selma says softly. "You see . . . Vince said he'd postpone his boys' weekend."

Straightaway Rahel says, "We'll do it."

□

She goes once around the entire farm looking for Peter.

He doesn't hear her coming. He's got his earbuds in and is singing in his wooden GDR English . . . *and love is not a victory march, it's a cold and it's a broken Hallelujah.*

As he sings he scatters chicken feed on the ground and is surrounded by the animals as if he's their king. The stork, his faithful companion, is standing outside the pen. Beside him sits the one-eared cat. The entire scene is absurd. Unreal, like an animated picture from a book of fairy tales.

The modern gadgetry is the only thing that's out of place. That and the bad singing.

Rahel discreetly slips away to avoid embarrassing him.

□

She goes from room to room but can't find any peace. The place has become too much for her. An impulse is telling her to get away from here. As quickly as possible. As if life had disappeared from this place too, as if Viktor, at the moment of his death, had sucked it out.

Rahel wanders around as if in a dream, touching objects, stroking dusty surfaces, rummaging in the collection of hundreds of records and, amongst one of the piles of books in the sitting room, finding a photo album.

In it there's a picture of Edith and Ruth. They're standing side by side on the shore of the lake, young, in long summer dresses. Ruth is a radiant beauty, but with the touch of cold that surrounds her perfection. Edith is beautiful too, but her face shows she's a broken woman and there's something skulking in her posture.

The future is already mapped out in both of them.

Saturday

When Rahel sees Ruth she has to compose herself to avoid sobbing out loud.

As ever Ruth is wearing her hair in a low bun, and her eyes and lips are tastefully made up, but the expression on her face . . .

As if it's frozen.

She greets Rahel and Peter with the hint of an embrace, takes a look around and asks a few questions without really being present. As she lets Peter carry her bags into the house she's surrounded by the cats but doesn't acknowledge any of them. Her eyes look big, wide open. Her firm, bare arms are tanned and she's wearing a long black dress.

Rahel says nothing.

Peter says, "Take your time."

Ruth goes into her and Viktor's bedroom.

□

At lunch, which she leaves untouched, Ruth's eyes keep wandering over to the studio. Taking sips from her water glass, she explains to them in a voice that sounds oddly different what will happen now. When the body will be transferred, her ideas for the funeral. She doesn't need any help, she insists. Frauke is coming for a few days and that will be enough.

Rahel and Peter should reckon on a funeral in a fortnight. She doesn't know if there will be enough space for them to stay in the house as she's expecting lots of people to come from a long way away.

A few cats slink around the table and Ruth's eyes move twitchily.

"Where's the cat with one ear?" she asks.

Peter looks around. "Haven't seen her since yesterday."

"He loved her the best," Ruth says.

□

After lunch she stands up and says, "Please excuse me."

Peter goes off to look for the cat.

Rahel leaps up, clears the table, hurries to her room and starts packing. The drawings are placed at the very bottom of her case, on top of them the clothes and books and anything else she no longer needs. She puts the cigarette and lighter in her handbag. Then she tidies up, gives the floor a quick mop, airs the room and goes one last time to the swimming spot where, spurred on by a sudden flush of courage, she swims all the way to the middle of the lake.

Floating on her back, her eyes closed, she thinks of the last seconds of Viktor's life.

Did he suffocate, like most people who drown? Or did his lungs fill with salty seawater? What was he thinking? Was he still able to think? Did he picture Rahel? Ruth? Or Edith? Or did panic extinguish all images and thoughts?

She turns and heads back to the shore. With powerful strokes she moves forwards, lies naked on the sand to dry, squints at the sun and is happy to be alive.

□

Later she goes with Peter on his last walk with the horse. His search for the cat was in vain. He seems gloomy and doesn't say much.

Baila walks close beside Peter, nudging him now and then on the shoulder, as if able to sense their imminent departure.

□

Not until supper do they all come together again, and none of them has any appetite. Ruth tells them how well they've looked after the garden, house and animals, saying that the place has rarely looked so neat and tidy. Then she immediately falls into another cold silence.

Vinegar flies gather in their wine glasses. Wasps cut tiny pieces from a slice of cooked ham and fly away with their booty. A spider crawls across the middle of the table.

One more night, Rahel thinks, just one more night.

"I'm going to have another look for the cat," Peter says out of the blue, then gets up and goes out.

The expression on Ruth's face is almost unbearable. Her inner despair is hidden behind an external mask, but its pull is so strong that Rahel spontaneously moves her chair a touch back from the table. And then, without warning, she asks the question.

She utters the shocking words as deadpan as possible, and when she says *father*, Ruth calmly looks her in the eye.

"I knew it would occur to you at some point," she says.

Rahel must have been around eight, Ruth says, when she first suspected. It was New Year 1978–79 when, after a snowstorm the like of which they'd never seen before, half the region was without electricity and tanks were mobilised to get supplies to people cut off from the outside world.

What Ruth then tells her tallies pretty accurately with Rahel's memory.

Viktor found the half-frozen girl behind a huge pile of snow in the yard. It was bitterly cold. She was sitting beside the exit to the cave they'd dug in the snow. Edith and Ruth thought Rahel was in one of the bedrooms upstairs. It didn't occur to either of them to check. Viktor was completely beside himself. Nobody knew how long Rahel had been sitting outside, but she was so small, slight and inadequately dressed that her body must have quickly become hypothermic. Her eyes were half closed and she wasn't moving when Viktor found her. He immediately lifted her up and brought her into the warm kitchen. Holding her tightly he screamed at Edith. Besides the anger there was something else in his face: naked fear.

"That evening I asked him straight out," Ruth says. After a few seconds, she adds, "He denied it." She raises her hands and lets them fall again. "By the way, it wasn't that bad. You didn't even get a cold."

"He denied it?" Rahel repeats. "Did you believe him?"

Ruth shrugs. "I wanted to." She sighs and her gaze turns inwards. Then she says, "When Edith went into the hospice, when you could still just about talk to her, I asked her as well. She looked at me, she looked at me for a long time. Then she said no and closed her eyes."

Rahel nods and cocoons herself in a silence in which she weighs up everything again. The questions, the answers, the credibility. And just as she's about to leave it for today, Ruth says, "He always wanted you to have the house one day. Perhaps that's enough of an answer."

They gaze at each other. There's nothing between them anymore. Ruth's eyes are empty with grief.

When Peter comes back in they've been sitting there for a long while in silence, both of them absorbed in their own memories.

The first thing Rahel notices is that he's bare-chested. Then she sees the bundle in his arms.

"You're not going to believe it," he says, laying the thing he's wrapped in his shirt on a chair beside Ruth. "She was behind the mirabelle tree." He opens the bundle.

The one-eared cat's jaws are slightly open. Her eyes are only half closed and the body is already stiff.

An icy shudder runs down Rahel's spine.

Ruth smiles. She places a hand on the dead animal and gives the faintest of nods.

Sunday

"Goodbye, my loves," Ruth says as they get into the car.

They slowly drive away. Ruth follows them as far as the boulder, with Mr Stork in tow a safe distance behind her.

For the first time she's standing there without Viktor, raising a hand and giving a little wave. Behind her the stork flaps its wings so fiercely that it lifts a few centimetres off the ground. It's almost flying.

Rahel is leaning over the headrest of her seat, calling out "Bye!" over and over again.

Tears are streaming down her face. She's waving like a woman possessed and she begins to sob.

Ruth is standing there as straight as a die. She doesn't have the energy for one last smile.

◻

Through Rahel's blurry eyes the countryside drifts past like an impressionist painting, and when they're beyond the village Peter puts his foot down. With the windows open they race down the long tree-lined road, the wind in their hair and smelling the dusty air of late summer. Rahel takes the cigarette from her handbag. The tobacco is now so dry that it's crumbling. Peter grins when she lights it.

He puts on the Gundermann CD, searches for her favourite song and when the chorus begins Rahel turns up the volume.

> . . . *the grass keeps growing*
> *tall, wild and green,*
> *until the scythes chop,*
> *quiet and serene.*

Acknowledgements

I would like to thank everyone who's helped make this book possible: my German publisher Philipp Keel, who once again had full confidence in my work; Ursula Bergenthal, who as editorial director was by my side with encouragement and advice; Ruth Geiger, who I could rely on for anything; and the rest of the Diogenes staff, who in their own way have played their part in the appearance of this novel.

Special thanks are due to my editor Kati Hertzsch. I'm very grateful for her expertise and her genuine pleasure at the work we've done together.

I'd like to thank my family for their support and my friends for the inspiration they've given me.

And thanks too to P. and T. for the summer days last year at their house by the lake. There, in a quiet moment, I sat at the desk, gazed out of the window for a while, unexpectedly had an idea and began to write the first few lines of this novel.

Quotations

p. v   From *An Essay on Man. An Introduction to a Philosophy of Human Culture* by Ernst Cassirer.

p. 48   From "Über den Wolken" by Reinhard Mey, who also wrote the lyrics. The song appeared on the 1974 album *Wie vor Jahr und Tag* with Intercor.

p. 108   From *Der Waldgang* by Ernst Jünger. Published in 2014 by J.G. Cotta'sche Buchhandlung Nachfolger GmbH, founded 1659, Stuttgart, p. 12.

p. 175   From "Hallelujah" by Leonard Cohen, who also wrote the lyrics. It appeared on the 1984 album *Various Positions* with Columbia. The Jeff Buckley cover version appeared on the 2007 album *Grace*, also with Columbia.

p. 182   Lines translated from "Gras" by Gerhard Gundermann, who also wrote the lyrics. It appeared on the 1992 album *Einsame Spitze* with BuschFunk.

DANIELA KRIEN was born in 1975 in Mecklenburg-Vorpommern, then in the G.D.R. Her first novel, *Someday We'll Tell Each Other Everything* (2013) was published in fifteen languages and has been made into a film directed by Emily Atef (Arte), a runner up for the "Golden Bear" award at the 2023 Berlin Film Festival. For a subsequent volume of short stories, *Muldental*, she was awarded the Nicolaus Born Prize. *Love in Five Acts* (2021) has been sold for translation into twenty languages and was on the German bestseller lists for many months. She lives in Leipzig with her two daughters.

JAMIE BULLOCH is the translator of novels by Arno Geiger, Robert Menasse, Timur Vermes and Birgit Vanderbeke, and crime fiction by Oliver Bottini, Sebastian Fitzek and Romy Hausmann. For Birgit Vanderbeke's *The Mussel Feast* he is a winner of the Schlegel-Tieck Prize.